What Goes Around

Look for the other books in this
inspirational series from Bantam Books.

clearwater crossing

What Goes Around

laura peyton roberts

BANTAM BOOKS
NEW YORK • TORONTO • LONDON • SYDNEY • AUCKLAND

RL 5.8, age 12 and up
WHAT GOES AROUND
A Bantam Book / October 2000

ISBN: 0-553-49330-2

Visit us on the Web! www.randomhouse.com/teens
Educators and librarians, for a variety of teaching tools, visit us at
www.randomhouse.com/teachers

Published simultaneously in the United States and Canada

Bantam Books is an imprint of Random House Children's Books, a
division of Random House, Inc. BANTAM BOOKS and the rooster
colophon are registered trademarks of Random House, Inc. Bantam
Books, 1540 Broadway, New York, New York 10036.

PRINTED IN THE UNITED STATES OF AMERICA

CWO 10 9 8 7 6 5 4 3 2 1

For in the same way you judge others, you will be judged, and with the measure you use, it will be measured to you.

Matthew 7:2

One

N icole Brewster rolled over in bed, pressing down
extra pillows and tangled sheets to check her
nightstand alarm clock.

Great, she thought unhappily. There were only
a few minutes left before the buzzer that Monday
morning, and even though she'd been inventing ex-
cuses for the last hour, she still hadn't come up with
one good enough to convince her mother to let her
stay home from school. She couldn't possibly *go,*
though—not after failing to get on the cheerleading
squad by just one position. Nicole had left school
crying the moment she'd found out on Friday, before
classes had even started, and by now she was sure to
be the laughingstock of the entire place.

None of her so-called friends had even phoned
her over the weekend. *Well, except for Courtney.
Kind of.*

The last thing Nicole had been in the mood for
was a dose of her best friend's putdowns, but it had
turned out Courtney wasn't even interested enough
in the fact that Nicole hadn't made cheerleader to

give her a hard time about it. She mentioned that she'd seen the list, throwing in a biting comment about one of the girls who had beaten Nicole, but mostly she'd just called to complain about the fact that Kyle Snowden hadn't asked her to the prom yet. Court thought it would be a good time for her and Nicole to come up with ideas for making him do it, since the prom was only a week away. Depressed, Nicole had told her friend she was watching a movie and then never called her back.

And technically I guess Melanie called too.

That call had come Sunday morning, though, when the other Brewsters were at church, so Nicole had been able to screen it with the answering machine. She wanted to talk to Melanie Andrews, the squad's new, not-even-a-junior-yet, cocaptain, even less than she wanted to talk to Courtney—although for different reasons. After Melanie had spent so much time coaching her on the sly, how could Nicole ever face her again, now that she'd failed? For that matter, how could she ever face anyone?

The alarm went off. Nicole slapped the button hard, but made no move to get up. *I'm just going to say I'm sick*, she decided. If mental illness counted, that wasn't even a lie.

Her mother must have anticipated her plan, though, because not five minutes later she came through the bedroom door.

"Rise and shine!" Mrs. Brewster said in a nauseatingly cheerful voice. Grabbing the cord, she pulled Nicole's curtains open with one cruel yank. "The birds are singing, the bees are buzzing, and it's bare-shoulder weather if I've ever seen it."

She herself was wearing a new sleeveless dress, her hair piled high and sprayed to perfection. The sun spilling through the window backlit her blond head like the flame on a tall thin candle.

"I'm sick." Nicole groaned, shielding her blood-shot eyes with one hand. "I think I have a fever."

"A fever?" Mrs. Brewster crossed to the bed and pressed the underside of her wrist to Nicole's forehead. "Nonsense. You just don't want to go to school. But I didn't make you go back on Friday *and* I let you stay home from church, so you've been sulking long enough. I know you're upset about this cheerleading thing, and I'm sorry. But you have to face up sometime."

"No I don't. There's only a month of school left, and we never learn anything now anyway. I could just stay out the rest of this year, and next year I could transfer to Ozarks Prep."

The suggestion left Nicole and her mother both staring, openmouthed. Clearwater Crossing, Missouri, only had one public high school, but even so, Nicole couldn't believe she had just proposed such a conservative Christian school as an alternative.

Despite the fact that her on-again, off-again boyfriend, Guy Vaughn, went there, Nicole couldn't see herself fitting in. If anything, Guy's attendance only made her proposal more shocking, since she and he were nothing alike, constantly falling out over stupid little things.

Mrs. Brewster was shocked for a different reason.

"Do you know how much that school costs?" she demanded. "And if we sent you, we'd have to send Heather. Your father and I looked into private school way back when, and it's just not going to happen, Nicole. You'll have to make due at CCHS."

Nicole received the news like an additional weight pinning her to the mattress. Tears pooled in her eyes at the thought of the humiliation that awaited.

"*Today*, Nicole," her mother said, yanking off the blankets. "You'd better be downstairs in fifteen minutes. I'm making blueberry pancakes."

Nicole's bare legs turned to gooseflesh as Mrs. Brewster strode out of the room, her sandal heels clicking down the stairs. Nicole hesitated a second, then forced herself up, afraid to risk another, even less pleasant, confrontation with her mother.

Unfortunately, the reflection she saw in her full-length mirror made her dread school even more. The harsh light streaming through her window only emphasized how swollen her eyes were from crying, and her shoulder-length hair looked like a bird's nest. Her legs were pale and stubbly beneath the ragged hem of her nightgown, and . . . was that a zit coming up on her chin? She looked awful. *Worse* than awful. She felt like the ugliest person on Earth.

"Oh boy. Pancakes," she said, her tears flowing over as she turned to dig through her dresser for something big and shapeless to wear. "I'm already Quasimodo and now she wants to make me fat, too."

"I'm glad I found you guys," Leah Rosenthal said.

There was plenty of room left at her friends' table on the edge of the quad. Smoothing her long skirt behind her legs, Leah dropped onto the seat beside Jenna Conrad. Peter Altmann sat across from Jenna, squinting into the sun, and Ben Pipkin had the seat beside him.

"Where's Miguel today?" Jenna asked as Leah tossed her brown bag onto the table. "I didn't see you guys Friday, either."

"Yeah, that's what I wanted to tell you." Opening her milk, Leah stuck a straw into the carton but then pushed it away. The events of the last few days had left her without much appetite. "Zachary Dewey died on Thursday, and Miguel was too upset to come to school. We spent most of Friday up at the lake."

"Zach died?" Jenna gasped.

"How?" Peter's blond hair spilled forward over disbelieving eyes as he leaned toward her across the table.

5

"That's awful," Ben said in the same instant. "Who's Zach?"

"A kid Miguel got to know working at the hospital," Leah answered. "He was only nine and he had kidney cancer."

"But I thought they got all the cancer out!" Peter said, his expression still stunned. "I thought he was going to be fine!"

"That's what everyone wanted to believe. But between the surgery, the chemo, and the radiation, Zach's poor little lungs couldn't take any more. Miguel is devastated."

"The poor guy," Jenna said tearfully. "That's so terrible."

"Please, *please* don't start crying," Leah begged, "or I'll end up crying again too. It feels like I've barely stopped."

"I can't help it," said Jenna, sniffling. She pushed her long brown hair back over one shoulder, then put her arm around Leah. "Are you okay?"

"Yeah. Sort of. Not so much." Leah swallowed hard, past the painful lump in her throat. "I will be," she said with a deep breath.

"What about Miguel?" Peter asked. "Weren't he and Zach really close?"

Leah nodded. "I'm worried about him. He said he was coming to school today, but he must have changed his mind."

"We should go to his house," Ben proposed. "Maybe he wants to talk about it."

Leah's eyebrows went up. "That's the last thing he wants," she said quickly, shaking her head. Someone else might think having his friends lend an ear was comforting—not Miguel. "He hates to talk about anything, and he can still barely stand to *think* about Zach."

She forced herself to drink some milk, trying to clear the block in her throat, but the hurt of the last few days seemed to have crystallized there like a stone.

"Well, we can at least go to the funeral with him," Ben persisted. "He doesn't have to talk if he doesn't want to, but he won't want to go to that alone."

Leah shook her head again. "The funeral was Friday. We saw the announcement in the paper."

"So soon?" Jenna asked with obvious amazement.

"Zach was Jewish," Leah explained. "The Jewish tradition is to bury people quickly, out of respect for the dead."

"But how did they make arrangements so fast?" Jenna persisted.

"I don't know," Leah answered. She didn't want to think about it, either. "All I know is, having Zach already buried just makes things worse for Miguel. It's like the whole thing is already over and Miguel still hasn't even admitted it's happened."

7

"I think it's kind of better," Ben said. "It's gross keeping bodies around for a week, making everyone look at them."

Leah felt the milk lurch in her stomach. "Well, it's not better for Miguel. And *please* don't give him your theories on that subject."

"He won't," Peter said, shooting Ben a warning look.

"We'll all be supersensitive when we talk to Miguel," Jenna promised.

"When you do, it's probably better not even to mention this," Leah warned. "Or just say something sympathetic that doesn't require a response. It's weird, I know, but it's how he is."

"I don't think it's weird," Peter said. "You get hurt enough times and after a while you're afraid to say things out loud."

Leah flashed him a weak smile, surprised by the depth of his understanding. Compared to all the things that had gone wrong in Miguel's life—his father's death, his mother's lengthy illness, and the family's subsequent financial ruin—Peter seemed to have the perfect, safe existence. For him to read Miguel so well showed a lot of empathy.

"We'll keep him and Zach in our prayers," Peter said. "And we'll fill in the rest of Eight Prime, so that nobody gives him the third degree. Tell Miguel we're thinking about him, though—and that we're here anytime he needs us."

"I will," Leah managed to force past the lump, giving up on not crying. Having her friends in Eight Prime—the group they'd formed last fall as a way to honor a classmate who had died—support her meant a lot. Especially now.

Jenna's arm tightened around Leah's shoulders as sympathetic tears slid down her cheeks too. "We're here for *both* of you," she whispered.

Finally! Melanie thought, spotting Nicole in the hall after sixth period. She'd been hunting for her unsuccessfully all day, but had guessed correctly that the other girl would at least have to stop by her locker before she left school. *I think that's Nicole anyway. What in the world is she wearing?*

Leaving the corner where she'd been keeping a lookout, Melanie wove hurriedly through the crowd. She had expected Nicole to be depressed about not making the cheerleading squad, so the fact that she hadn't returned her call on Sunday hadn't surprised her much. The fact that Nicole was nowhere to be seen at lunchtime hadn't even surprised her much. But the baggy drawstring pants and potato sack of a top Nicole was wearing surprised her a lot, almost more than the fact that Nicole's usual layers of makeup were missing. The only color she seemed to be wearing was a too-orange dot of concealer over a gathering zit on her chin.

"I've been looking for you everywhere!" Melanie

complained, leaning against a nearby locker. "And what's up with the outfit? If you're trying out grunge, you're a little late."

Nicole gave her a wounded look, then quickly glanced away. "I didn't feel like dressing up."

"Obviously."

The traffic wasn't as thick as it had been a few minutes before, but there were still plenty of people to overhear them. Grabbing Nicole by one shoulder, Melanie closed her locker and steered her into the nearest vacant classroom. "Look, I know how you feel," she said, shutting the door behind them.

"No you don't," Nicole returned sullenly.

Maybe she had a point. Melanie had breezed onto the cheerleading squad as a sophomore, and making it again this year had proven even less challenging. There was no way she could claim she'd worked as hard for the honor as Nicole, who had practiced and worried until she'd made them both crazy.

"Okay, maybe I don't. But I can guess. Besides, runner-up is not that bad. It's nothing to be ashamed of."

Perching on the edge of a desk, Melanie waited for Nicole to take a seat beside her. "The thing is, you have to hold your head up, Nicole. A lot of things could happen between now and fall. All it's going to take is for one girl to drop out."

"Who's going to drop out?" Nicole demanded. "No one would be that stupid."

"I'm just saying, things change. You never know. But in the meantime you shouldn't be acting beaten—you should be acting like you're already on the squad. If you want to be a cheerleader, look like cheerleader material."

Melanie knew she was right, but she braced for an argument anyway. She and Nicole didn't have the smoothest history, and even though the two of them had been getting along pretty well lately, they still weren't exactly best friends. It wasn't as if they bared their souls to each other, or even talked about anything besides cheerleading and Eight Prime. No matter how much time they spent together, neither of them could seem to forget the beginning of the school year, when Nicole's futile crush on Jesse Jones had turned her against Melanie at every opportunity.

So Melanie couldn't have been more amazed when Nicole slumped over against her shoulder, buried her face in her hands, and burst into tears.

"I *am* beaten," she cried. "I'm such a loser. The whole school knows I wasn't good enough to make the squad—two years in a row!"

"No, they don't. And I'm sure they must have better things to think about. Cheerleading just isn't that big a deal."

11

Nicole lifted her tear-streaked face long enough to shoot her an incredulous, miserable look.

"It isn't," Melanie insisted. "Besides, the new squad doesn't even start performing until next year. Before that there's the prom, and graduation, and summer camp with the Junior Explorers." She was careful not to mention cheerleading camp. "Who are you going to the prom with? Guy?"

The question seemed harmless enough, but it only made Nicole cry harder.

"Guy and I always argue. Besides, I wanted someone to ask *me*." Pausing for a big, shuddery breath, Nicole drew her sleeve across her runny nose. "I thought if I made cheerleader, the boys would be lining up. But now . . ."

She broke down again, crying so hard that Melanie was at a loss. For Nicole to be so openly brokenhearted over something so trivial showed a total lack of pride. Unless she and Nicole were actually friends now . . .

"You could get a date easily," Melanie said, putting a tentative hand on Nicole's shoulder. Nicole didn't pull away. "If you don't want to go with Guy, why *not* ask someone else?"

"I—I couldn't," Nicole got out. "Everyone normal already has a date." Wriggling closer, she burrowed her wet face into Melanie's shoulder.

"That's just not the case," Melanie said, her heart

contracting painfully at the truth of her own words. "There are still good people out there, looking."

"How do you know?"

"I just know, all right?"

She had no intention of discussing Friday's disaster, when Jesse had arrived at her house unexpectedly and—even more unexpectedly—asked her to the prom. For one thing, she and Jesse would probably always be a touchy subject with Nicole. More importantly, she didn't want to think about it herself.

If only he'd given me some sort of hint! she thought for the millionth time. *Just something. Anything. I'd have never said yes to Steve if I'd known there was any chance that Jesse—*

"Who are you going with?" Nicole sniffled into Melanie's sleeve. "I mean, somebody asked *you.* Right?"

"Steve Carson. I don't think you know him—he's in my art class."

Nicole lifted her head a little. "I've seen him around. He's cute."

"He is." But Melanie's voice must have lacked enthusiasm.

"What's wrong with him?" Nicole asked suspiciously.

"Nothing! Nothing's wrong with him. All I'm saying is, you ought to ask someone. There are lots of Steves out there."

For a moment, Melanie actually considered mentioning the fact that Jesse didn't have a date, but she disregarded the notion almost as quickly as it occurred to her. Even if she and Nicole were having some sort of relationship breakthrough, it didn't have to include handing her Jesse on a plate.

Besides, maybe there's still some way I can go with him.

Not that she'd been able to think of one so far—and she'd been thinking of little else. If only he had let her explain the situation before he'd stormed off Friday night. He hadn't listened past "no," though, so she hadn't been able to tell him that the only reason she hadn't leapt at his offer was that she'd already promised Steve. She hadn't spoken to him since then, and since she still hadn't figured out what to say when she did, she hadn't gone looking for him, either.

If only there were some nice way to get out of going with Steve!

Up until lunchtime that Monday, she had still held out a glimmer of hope that Steve wasn't locked into taking her, that if she explained things to him he might be just as happy going with someone else. That was before he'd shown up at her cafeteria table with a smile and a pink carnation. By the time he'd finally moved on, the entire cheerleading squad and half the football players knew they were going together—and that was on top of

14

all the other people Steve had already told. There was just no way to make the switch now without completely embarrassing him, and he didn't deserve that.

You're the one who led him on, Melanie reminded herself. *He's never been anything but sweet to you.*

If she dropped him now, the whole school would find out. And what if he couldn't get another date? Despite what she'd just told Nicole, it wasn't going to be easy to ask someone on such short notice.

On the other hand, he is only a junior. He can always go next year.

That seemed a bit hypocritical, though. By the time she was a senior, Melanie would have gone to CCHS's Junior/Senior Prom all four years, since only one person in the couple had to be old enough.

"I don't even care about the prom!" Nicole declared miserably, dropping her head back to Melanie's shoulder. "All I wanted was to be a cheerleader, and now I never, ever will!"

For a moment, Melanie thought of escape. She obviously wasn't doing Nicole any good, so if she just patted her on the back a few times, maybe she could slip away. And maybe, if she hurried, she could still catch Jesse in the parking lot. She'd tell him how much she wished she could go with him, and this time she'd *make* him listen. . . .

Except how could she do that when Nicole had a death grip on her sleeve?

With a sigh, Melanie rubbed her friend's back and made a few soothing noises. Nicole had to be really distraught to show her feelings so openly.

And I do feel sorry for her.

More than that, she suddenly realized, she felt guilty. If she hadn't filled Nicole's head with false hope, if she hadn't coached her to within one place of making the squad, failure would have happened earlier and been a lot less painful. But instead she had interfered, and now, in a way, this was all her fault.

If only I'd coached her better. If we had just run through that original dance maybe five or six more times . . . Or maybe it was my choreography.

She had done her best, but there were better choreographers on the squad. Tanya Jeffries, for instance.

I could have asked Tanya to help.

Nicole continued to cry, oblivious to Melanie's second thoughts. With a sigh, Melanie put her other arm around her and hugged her.

"That's all right," she said. "We'll get you onto the squad somehow."

Nicole kept crying, but Melanie felt better. After all, she was a cocaptain now—maybe there were some strings she could pull with Sandra, their coach. Or maybe one of the new girls would turn out to be unexpectedly bad and have to be replaced. Could

Sandra do that after she'd already made the announcement? Would she?

Melanie squeezed Nicole again, but her mind was far away. Injuries, bad grades, a family leaving town—there were a lot of things that could happen between now and fall.

I'll just have to make sure something does.

Two

"Finally!" sighed Miguel, walking gratefully through his front door.

School that Tuesday had been even more of an ordeal than he had anticipated. Most people had absolutely no idea about Zach, of course, but it was still completely bizarre to see them carrying on with their lives, smiling and laughing and having a good time. The upcoming prom at the Lakehouse Lodge was the big subject on most people's minds—something which seemed both weird and awful under the circumstances. How could people care about things like high school dances when there were nine-year-olds dying of cancer? What was wrong with the world?

At least when Kurt Englbehrt had died at the beginning of the school year, Miguel hadn't felt like the only one who cared. The whole student body had been hurt by that loss because they had all known Kurt. But this time Miguel was alone. Leah was the only one who understood, and even she couldn't completely share his pain.

"I shouldn't have bothered going. What difference does it make?" he muttered, dropping his backpack on the living room floor and wandering into the kitchen.

A note on the dinette said his sister Rosa was spending the afternoon at a friend's house. With his mother still at work, that meant he'd have a couple of hours to himself before anyone came home.

Good, he thought. His mother and younger sister were full of sympathy about Zach, but not only was sympathy useless, hearing it wore him out. He wouldn't mind being alone for a while.

Grabbing a soda out of the refrigerator, he walked back to the living room and collapsed on the sofa, popping the cold can open and rolling it back and forth between his palms. It felt strange not to be leaving for work at the hospital, but he hadn't set foot in the place since he'd learned Zach died, and he didn't intend to ever again. Miguel knew he ought to go back and officially quit, but he just couldn't force himself to do it.

Besides, when a person runs off his job in the middle of a shift, then skips the next few days without a word, it's pretty obvious what's going on. I think Dr. Wells will figure it out.

Still, it felt weird not to be dressing for work. Reaching for the remote, Miguel flipped on the TV. He had a bunch of homework to do, and he'd promised Leah he'd call her, but there was time for all of that later. Now that he wasn't working anymore, there was almost too much time.

I could always go see Mr. Ambrosi. Miguel's former boss had promised to put him back on a construction crew anytime he wanted.

Leah would love that.

After the aggressive move Mr. Ambrosi's daughter, Sabrina, had made on him, Miguel wasn't too sure he was up for it himself. On the other hand, the contractor ran multiple crews; Miguel could always ask not to work on Sabrina's.

Except that explaining why might get kind of tricky.

Besides, shouldn't I be able to handle Sabrina myself? I already told her I'm not interested. It's not like she's going to jump me. I don't think.

He was still pondering the situation when a loud, unexpected knock at his front door made him spill a ribbon of Coke down the front of his shirt.

"Great," he muttered, slapping at the liquid as he struggled to his feet. "Who the heck is that?"

When Miguel opened the door and found Howard standing there, he almost dropped the soda altogether. The pediatric nurse was wearing scrubs, a stethoscope looped back over his shoulder as if he were still on duty. The man's crewcut bristled with its usual prickliness, but Howard's eyes were sympathetic as he took a long look at Miguel.

"You've got something on your shirt," he said.

20

Miguel rubbed at the wet stain. "I know."

Howard shifted his weight on the del Rioses' small doorstep, his eyes dropping to focus on the paper bag in his hands. Miguel wondered if he should invite him in, then just as quickly wondered how to get out of it. He liked Howard all right, but they had nothing in common except their work at the hospital—and that was the last thing Miguel wanted to talk about.

"I brought you something," Howard said abruptly, shoving the paper bag forward. "Mrs. Dewey came by yesterday. She wanted to give you this in person, but since you weren't there, I said I'd make sure you got it."

Miguel took the bag reluctantly and let it dangle from one hand, unopened. He couldn't imagine what Zach's mother had brought him—and he didn't want to look.

"It's a book," Howard said, reading his mind. "And a card. And the Wildcats hat you gave Zach. She wanted you to have something to remember him by."

Miguel could feel his throat constricting. His eyes burned with the effort of holding back tears. "Okay. Well. Thanks."

"You're welcome."

Miguel started to push the door shut, but Howard stopped it with one quick hand. "We were also wondering when we'd see you at work again. Dr. Wells isn't angry—he knows you've been through a real

21 22 2339

tough time. But you can't just walk off a job like that, Miguel. People are counting on you, and we need to know your plans."

"Just . . . *don't* count on me," Miguel forced out. "I'm not coming back."

"Ever?" Howard looked amazed. "You don't mean ever."

Howard's genuine surprise almost made Miguel reconsider. But how could he go back there now? After what had happened?

"I can't," he said. "You'd better find someone else."

Howard took a step away from the door, then stood hesitating on the doorstep. "You probably think we don't know what you're going through, but we do. We've all been through it. And not just with Zachary, either. The first one you lose hurts the worst, though. Believe it or not, it does get easier."

"Well, it shouldn't!" Miguel said angrily. "There shouldn't be anything easy about it!"

"Doctors and nurses are only human," Howard said quietly. "No matter how hard we try, we can't save everyone. Sometimes you just have to tell yourself you did your best and focus on your victories."

If Howard was trying to make things better, he was only making them worse. Miguel wasn't about to gloss over what had happened, to say Zach's death was okay because it couldn't be helped. *Why* couldn't it be helped? That was the question people ought to be asking.

Was he the only one who understood how wrong this whole thing was?

"Okay. I have to go now," he said, trying to push the door shut again.

"Just think about what I said," Howard insisted. "Take a couple more days, then give Dr. Wells a call. I'll tell him you're going to."

"Fine," said Miguel, succeeding in closing the door at last.

Howard could tell Dr. Wells whatever he wanted. That didn't mean it was going to happen.

"Ooh, Jenna! You look like a princess!" Sarah Conrad exclaimed, pressing her small hands together. She leaned forward on the living room sofa, her cane sliding forgotten to the floor. "I wish I had a dress like that!"

"You will someday," Jenna said happily, twirling around just to see her skirt swirl out. "Wait until *you* go to prom."

Jenna and her mother had just arrived home from the mall, where Jenna had put the dress on layaway over the weekend. She'd fallen so in love with it that she'd put down all her saved allowance on the spot. That had barely covered half the price, though, and it had taken until that Tuesday afternoon to convince her mother to pay for the rest.

"It's not that I object to buying you a dress," Mrs. Conrad had said over and over. "But does it have to

23

be so ridiculously expensive? We could find another dress with shoes for just my half, and you could keep your money."

It was worth every penny, Jenna thought now as she modeled for her sisters. The dress's strapless satin bodice was the palest shade of pink, with layers of matching netting spilling down over a long, full skirt. Even wearing it with her sneakers made her feel like a queen. She imagined her long hair up, a handful of crystals scattered through it, and just a touch of glitter on her bare shoulders.

"It's awfully girlie," said Maggie, breaking into her reverie. "Didn't it come in black?"

"I didn't *want* black," Jenna began irritably, but before she could say any more the rest of her sisters shouted Maggie down.

"No, not black!" Sarah said, horrified. "The pink is so pretty."

"I like it too," said Allison, in a surprising show of independence. Ever since she and Maggie had started sharing a bedroom, they had become two sides of the same coin.

"That dress is gorgeous," Caitlin proclaimed, getting the final word. "And it's absolutely perfect for you."

"That's what I think too," Jenna said, tossing Maggie a triumphant look. "I'm going to call Peter and tell him I got it."

Running up the two flights of stairs to the bedroom

24

she shared with Caitlin was no easy trick with that much fabric around her legs, but Jenna managed to do it without tripping. Alone on the third floor, she took one more twirl in front of the mirror before reluctantly removing the dress and hooking its ribbon loops over a hanger. Instead of putting the hanger in the closet, though, she hung it over the back of the door so she could admire the gown while she pulled on some jeans and a sweatshirt. Then she picked up her phone and dialed Peter.

"I got my dress!" she said, the second he answered. "Wait until you see it."

"I could come over now," Peter offered.

"No! You can't see it until Saturday night." Skipping across the room, she ran the netting between her fingers. "It's pink, and that's all I'm saying."

"Long or short?"

"Long."

"Sleeves or strapless?"

"Pink! That's all I'm saying," she scolded, giggling.

"I'm just trying to figure out what type of corsage to get you. You don't want me pinning it onto bare skin, do you?"

He had a point.

"Get a wrist corsage, and you'll be safe either way," she told him. "And that's really all I'm saying."

Jenna knew that some girls coordinated their clothes with their dates', matching the guys' ties and cummerbunds to the exact shade of their dresses, but she wanted Peter to be surprised when he saw her. Besides, she couldn't picture him in a pink tie anyway.

"Well, if you don't want to talk about the prom, then how about camp?" Peter said. "We still have a ton of things to do for that."

"I know. I've been trying to make up a name, and I think I finally have one. How about Camp Runamok?"

"Very funny."

"It *is* funny!" she insisted. "The kids will love it."

"If they get it. But it might not inspire much confidence on the part of their parents. I think we'd better keep trying."

"I guess. If you say so."

Jenna had really liked her idea, but the camp was for the Junior Explorers, and the Junior Explorers were Peter's project. Now that things were back to normal after their recent fight, she'd been helping him more than ever, but the final decisions were still made by him and his partner, Chris Hobart.

"We don't need to decide on a name right now anyway," Peter said. "I'm a lot more worried about working up a schedule to make sure we have enough counselors to cover the whole summer."

"Shouldn't we do the activities schedule before the counselor schedule? Like Monday fishing, Tuesday baseball, or whatever?"

"It's essentially all the same schedule. And it's

going to be more complicated than that, because we need at least four activities every day."

"Four?" Jenna repeated, a bit overwhelmed.

"Unless we go on a field trip, or something else that takes a long time. Otherwise, two things before lunch and two after sounds about right. Those little kids have short attention spans."

"How are we going to come up with twenty new things every week?"

"We aren't," Peter said calmly. "We'll have swimming every day, and we can do arts and crafts two or three times per week. Fishing maybe twice a week. Hikes once or twice. Sports. It ought to fill itself in. Plus, if we work out a good schedule the first month, we can use it over again twice, to take us to the end of the summer."

"Oh. Good idea."

"The hardest thing will probably be coming up with ideas for arts and crafts, because that *will* have to be different every time."

"We can always ask the Sunday school teachers to share ideas with us," Jenna said. "Plus there are books galore for that sort of thing."

"Do you want to see if you can find some?" he asked. "Maybe you can be in charge of planning all the crafts. We'll call you Art Director or something."

"Okay," Jenna agreed, liking her new title. Not only that, but she was flattered to be asked instead of

Melanie, since everyone knew who the real artist in the group was. "I'll stop by the school library tomorrow morning and see what they have."

"If you find anything good, bring it to lunch. Do you want to meet at our usual table?"

"All right," she said happily.

But within a minute of hanging up, she had forgotten about lunch, forgotten about the library, and even forgotten about Art Director. Her thoughts went straight back to the prom.

"I should try that dress on with all my good shoes," she said.

After all, if none of them looked perfect, she'd have to borrow a pair from her mom, or Caitlin. Or maybe she'd have to go shopping again.

Jenna peeled her sweatshirt off over her head as she headed for the closet. "This is going to be so fun!"

"So *why* are you here?" Charlie Johnson asked Jesse. The old man looked even more frail than the last time Jesse had seen him, but his gaze was still as piercing as he leaned over the TV tray in front of his shabby recliner. "With a face like that, it can't be to cheer me up."

"I told you," Jesse said sullenly, slouching on the equally shabby brown sofa. "I thought you might want to do some grocery shopping."

"If I'd known you were coming, I could have made a list."

Jesse opened his mouth to say something rude—like, how hard can it be to remember an orange and a can of soup?—then snapped it shut again. He didn't actually care if they went to the store or not.

"If you don't want to go, that's fine with me. It was just an idea."

"Uh-huh," Charlie said knowingly. "I've barely seen you since Christmas, and suddenly my groceries are your top priority? Did my son send you over here?"

"What? No, of course not."

Although it was true that the first time Jesse had gotten involved with Charlie, it was because Coach Davis had forced him into helping as part of a forty-hour community service sentence for bringing liquor to school. At first Jesse had had no idea why the coach was picking on him, making him chore boy to some random senior citizen on top of the suspension he'd already endured. But when Charlie had revealed his own alcoholic past, Jesse had begun to suspect the coach's choice wasn't so random. He had still been shocked, however, when he'd finally learned the truth—that CCHS's football coach was Charlie's estranged only son. The two men didn't even have the same last name anymore, since the coach had switched to his stepfather's.

"Are you, uh . . . are you and Coach speaking again?" Jesse dared to ask.

Charlie shrugged his bent shoulders. "Not unless you know something I don't."

"Sorry." Did the old guy look disappointed? Jesse couldn't tell.

"So you're only here for the pleasure of my fascinating company?"

"I just thought . . . I mean . . . Yeah. Something like that."

The truth was, Jesse wanted someone to commiserate with him over Melanie's heartless treatment, but the situation was so embarrassing that he couldn't bring himself to mention it to his family or anyone his own age. He knew now, though, that he couldn't mention it to Charlie, either. It was simply too humiliating, to admit how he'd swallowed his pride for Melanie again just to have her walk all over him.

Again.

Was he crazy to have thought she was hinting about the prom? He certainly hadn't rushed in like a fool—however foolish she'd made him look. If she hadn't wanted him to ask her, then why had she made such a point of letting him know she was available? Could he have misread her signals—or was she just playing with his head? And speaking of heads, was he ever going to get out of his? Or was he doomed to waste his entire life still wanting her, dreaming of holding her in his arms again? . . .

Forget it, stupid. She doesn't want you.

"All right," Charlie said, leaning back with a calculating look. "Since we're not going shopping

30

and you don't want to talk, how about painting my house?"

"Excuse me?" Jesse thought he must have misheard.

"Not the inside. Just the exterior."

"*Excuse* me?" Now he was *hoping* he had misheard.

"I'm just saying, if you don't have anything more productive to do than hang around here, maybe you'd like to paint the house."

"I don't think so."

A trace of slyness came over Charlie's face. "Fine. I just thought maybe you could use a hundred dollars."

"A hundred dollars?" For painting the entire exterior of a two-story, all-wood house? He'd known Charlie was cheap, but he hadn't known he was crazy. "A hundred bucks wouldn't even cover the paint!"

Charlie blinked. "Well, a hundred dollars plus the paint. That's what I meant. Obviously."

Is he serious? Jesse wondered. *This house could be in "Psycho" and a hundred dollars is barely gas money.*

For me, he realized a moment later. *Charlie doesn't even buy catsup without a coupon. How's he going to afford a hundred bucks?*

The old guy must be pretty desperate to offer that kind of money. Especially since when the paint, brushes, putty, and who-knew-what-else got added up, the number would probably triple. Jesse had no desire to paint Charlie's house—not even for decent money. But if he said no, who would do it? No sane

31

person would even *look* at the job for less than a thousand dollars.

He was starting to wish he'd never come over.

"Charlie," he said, half whining. "What do I know about painting houses?"

"So you'll learn by doing!" Charlie said triumphantly. "What a great opportunity for you! When do you want to start?"

"Why are you so hot on having your house painted anyway? You never even go outside."

Charlie nodded. "True. But you gotta keep paint on the wood or eventually it rots out."

A little late for that. But Jesse kept the thought to himself. The last thing he wanted was to give the guy more ammunition.

"It's just that I'm pretty busy now, with school and everything."

"That's all right. I don't mind if you do it in the afternoons and on weekends."

"Charlie . . ."

The old man obviously wasn't going to take a hint, and Jesse didn't have the heart to tell him no outright. "Fine. I'll do it. Are you happy?"

"Me? *You're* the one who's making the hundred bucks."

"Oh. Right. I'd better go call my stockbroker."

On the drive home, Jesse tried to figure out why he'd agreed to such an awful deal. He mostly felt sorry for Charlie, he guessed. And the old guy *had* helped him through a pretty rough time.

"Well, we ought to be even after this," he muttered, taking a corner too fast. "We ought to be *more* than even."

On the other hand, it wasn't as if his social life was so busy. If he heard one more thing about the prom . . .

I'll start tomorrow, he decided.

Anything to take his mind off Melanie.

Three

"As you all know, it's Principal Appreciation Day," Vanessa Winters told the lunchtime crowd in the quad.

Standing between football captain Hank Lundgreen and Principal Kelly on the dais erected for the festivities, Vanessa clutched the microphone with red-tipped fingers, her chin lifted with a sense of her own importance. Melanie watched passively from the concrete with the rest of the old cheering squad, trying to keep her dislike for their leader from showing on her face.

"This year the student council, the cheerleaders, and the sports teams have all pitched in to show Principal Kelly how much everyone here at CCHS appreciates his hard work and guidance," Vanessa continued, in a nauseatingly smarmy tone of voice. She turned to Principal Kelly with a big, fake smile. "On behalf of the entire student body, it is my pleasure to present you with this year's principal appreciation gift."

She waved one hand dramatically, and a black leather desk chair sporting a red bow levitated up to the dais, propelled by the trio of guys underneath. Melanie joined in the lackluster applause, until somebody yelled "No speech!" prompting genuine cheers.

With a grin, Principal Kelly dropped into the chair and spun around, his feet sticking out like a little kid's. Hank got in on the act and began spinning the chair until Vanessa made him stop, earning a few scattered boos. At last, the principal stood again and reeled up to the microphone, his balance showing the effects of all that spinning.

"Thank you," he said giddily. "As always, it is an honor being your principal, and I especially like the part where you buy me stuff. On behalf of all of me, my thanks to all of you."

There was some more applause, then the chant started from the back: "Dunk him, dunk him, dunk him!"

Vanessa's expression changed from sticky sweet to slightly evil before she finally bent to retrieve the foil-covered crown and scepter the cheerleaders had made. She placed the crown on the principal's head, and Hank led him out a plank extending from the dais to a "throne" suspended over a giant tub of water. The principal took his seat and waved his scepter regally, pretending ignorance of his impending fate.

Splash! Hank pulled a lever and Principal Kelly dropped into the water below, the noise of his impact all but drowned by the tumult of cheers from the crowd. At last he came up dripping, waving his now-limp scepter, and the ritual was complete. CCHS's long-suffering principal had been "appreciated" enough for one more year.

"What are you doing now?" Tanya Jeffries asked Melanie as the crowd began to break up. "Do you want to get some lunch? Or are you eating with Steve?"

"No, I'm not eating with Steve." Melanie's voice came out more annoyed than she had intended. "I don't even know where he is," she added, more normally.

"He must be here somewhere. Everybody is."

Tanya stood on her toes to scan the crowd, but Melanie grabbed her friend's red sweater and pulled her back down to her heels.

"That's all right. I'm sure I'll run into him eventually," she said, trying hard not to sound negative. It was just that Steve was developing a definite habit of showing up wherever she went lately, which wasn't a good thing. When Jesse had crowded her the same way it had made her crazy—and she was in love with Jesse.

Jesse, she thought with a silent groan. There was the person she really wanted to find. Here it was, already Wednesday, and she still hadn't talked to him about last Friday. She hadn't talked to him at all.

I'm sure he's asked someone else to the prom by now. Or else someone has asked him.

Still, shouldn't she at least *try* to explain? After all, the prom was just for one night, and there was nothing to keep them apart after that.

Nothing but fear and pride, anyway.

"You know what? I'm not really hungry," Melanie told Tanya. "I'm just gonna run by my locker and get that orange I didn't eat yesterday."

"You don't want to eat with Vanessa," Tanya guessed, grinning.

"That too."

Waving good-bye to her fellow cocaptain, Melanie took off across the crowded quad in search of Jesse. He'd been missing at lunch the last three days, so she figured he was avoiding her, but intuition told her she might find him down at the gym. Sure enough, his bright red BMW was parked in the lot out front. Jesse was reclining lazily behind the wheel, a sandwich in one hand.

Melanie heard music from the open driver's window as she walked cautiously over the asphalt, half-afraid to jolt him out of his reverie. She made it almost to the car before he noticed her, but when he did, he snapped to attention so quickly that he dropped his sandwich in his lap, then hurriedly brushed it off onto the floor in an obvious attempt to appear casual. She thought his reaction was kind of cute—until he opened his mouth.

"What are *you* doing here?" he demanded nastily. "What do you want?"

"I don't want anything," she said, taken aback.

"Then why are you here?" He jabbed a finger at his CD player, finding the Off button without shifting his glare from Melanie's face. "Can't a guy get a little peace?"

"I didn't realize you were meditating," she said caustically. "If you're out here solving world hunger or something, I can come back later." She narrowed her eyes to match his. "Or not."

"Suit yourself. You always do."

"What's that supposed to mean?"

"I'm just saying."

"Saying *what*?"

"You know what."

"All I know is that I came over here like a perfectly normal human being, and you're jumping down my back for no reason."

"No reason?" Jesse shouted, rising up until his thighs hit the steering wheel. "I think I have a fine reason! You can't have it both ways, Melanie. You can't flirt with me one day and blow me off the next. I'm not a . . . a girl!"

Melanie felt her mouth drop open. For a moment, all she could do was blink.

"Oh, that's right. You can treat a *girl* any way you want, but we're all supposed to kiss up to *guys*," she said, her voice dripping sarcasm. "You know what? That's exactly the attitude that made me break up with you in the first place."

"Like I care!" he exclaimed. "That's so over."

"Yeah? It wasn't over Friday, when you asked me to the prom."

The veins stood out in Jesse's neck, and when he finally spoke again his voice had dropped to a rasp. "You were the one dropping hints right and left, like you couldn't get a date. I felt sorry for you."

"You what?" Melanie said, stunned.

Jesse shrugged. "What did you think?"

Here was her chance to explain—except that her heart was thumping so hard she could barely breathe. Part of her felt like she might be sick as she tried to make sense of what was happening. Should she tell him how she felt? She was still so angry with him she could barely remember how that was.

"Jesse, I—"

"There you are, Melanie!" a cheerful voice broke in. "I've been looking all over for you."

She wheeled around to find Steve Carson standing behind her, his pale hair nearly white in the sunshine and a friendly smile reaching up into his blue eyes.

"Steve!" she said.

"Hey, Jesse," Steve said calmly, apparently unaware that his timing couldn't be worse.

"Do I know you?" Jesse asked rudely.

Melanie squeezed her eyes shut, then slowly opened them again, afraid to look and afraid not to.

"I guess not. Steve Carson." He stepped forward to shake Jesse's hand through the open window. "I know you from our football games."

Jesse didn't move a muscle, but the expression on his face . . .

"Well! So!" Melanie intervened brightly, hurriedly grabbing both of Steve's hands and spinning his back toward Jesse. "What did you need me for?"

Steve smiled. "I don't *need* you. I just wanted you."

Jesse snorted.

"For what?" she asked, feeling the crimson creep up her cheeks.

"No reason." For the first time Steve looked a little uncertain. "Am I, uh—am I interrupting something?"

Melanie squeezed his hands and glanced nervously past him to Jesse. She was seriously tempted to tell them both the truth. . . .

Then Jesse sneered and looked away.

"No," she said, her voice as cool as she could make it. "You're not interrupting anything at all. Did you get your tuxedo yet?"

"Yes. And my dad rented us a limo, too."

She could see Jesse's left ear turn red, but that was as much of his face as was showing.

Serves him right, she thought. *It's not like I owe him an explanation. Especially not if he's going to be such a jerk.*

"Come on," she said, pulling Steve away from the car toward the cafeteria. "There are still a few minutes before the bell rings, and I haven't eaten yet. Let's grab something fast, and you can tell me all about it."

"Sure," he said eagerly. "It's going to be black, with a little refrigerator and a TV and . . ."

Melanie didn't even glance back over her shoulder as she walked off with Steve. She had clearly read way too much into Jesse asking her to the prom. If anything, Steve's interruption had just kept her from making an enormous fool of herself.

Besides, if Jesse didn't like her, then Steve clearly did. His words tumbled over each other as he described every detail of the limo and the restaurant he planned to take her to. He was so sweet, so genuinely enthusiastic. She couldn't imagine him ever being nasty, or stubborn, or egotistical, or any of the rude things Jesse was.

Closing the small gap between them, she slipped her hand into his back pocket. He blushed a little, but the smile on his face stretched from ear to ear.

"We're going to have a killer time Saturday," he said. "I promise."

* * *

"He asked me!" Courtney crowed, sneaking up in the hall after school on Wednesday and yanking down on Nicole's backpack.

The tug was so hard and unexpected that it almost pulled Nicole off her platforms. She only managed to stay upright by grabbing Courtney's arm and stumbling backward until her shoes were underneath her again.

"Who asked you what?" she said resignedly, resuming her walk to her locker.

But she already knew. All week Courtney had been going back and forth on the subject of whether or not she should ask Kyle to the prom. She couldn't understand why he hadn't already asked her, and with every day that passed, the problem became more urgent. One minute she swore she was going to ask him, the next she wanted to wait for him to ask her, and the next she wanted to go with someone else entirely. Nicole thought the truth was that Courtney was *afraid* to ask him, since the dance was already so close and he hadn't so much as mentioned it. His failure to bring it up didn't necessarily mean he just didn't like dancing, either. What if he was going with someone else? With Kyle, anything was possible.

"Kyle asked me! We're going!" Courtney said delightedly. "You *have* to go to the prom now, Nicole, because we have to go shopping together! When are you going to call Guy?"

Nicole reached her locker and wearily began

spinning the combination. As usual, the only person Courtney cared about was herself. Nicole couldn't get the pain and humiliation of not making cheerleader out of her mind, but now that Courtney had a date to the prom Nicole was just supposed to forget everything and ask Guy so that the two of them could go shopping? Courtney didn't even care that Nicole and Guy had argued, or that being the one who had to ask was completely embarrassing. She didn't seem to realize that simply getting through the last few days had been murder, and that Nicole could have really used a best friend to lean on. Instead, Court had been chasing Kyle all over campus, doing whatever she could think of to entice him into giving her her way. If Courtney could just have supported her a little, or even shown some sympathy . . . but apparently that was asking too much.

"I don't even know if I want to go, let alone with Guy," Nicole said with a sigh. "But even assuming I asked him, you know there's no way we can double. Right? No way am I putting Guy and Kyle in the same limousine."

Or you and Guy, for that matter, she added silently. There was just too much history there, most of it bad. Guy and Jeff were friends. Courtney and Jeff used to be boyfriend and girlfriend. Courtney didn't like Guy. Jeff no longer liked Courtney. Jeff *did* like Hope, his new girlfriend. And nobody really liked Kyle—not even Courtney, when she was honest.

"Don't worry," Courtney scoffed. "I have no intention of hanging out with the God Squad on prom night."

"Oh, so now Guy's in the God Squad too?"

"Please!" Courtney waved one dismissive hand. "He could be their leader. No, Kyle and I have bigger things planned. A real *romantic* evening."

Nicole didn't want to know what Kyle's idea of romance was. It probably involved getting drunk and slipping his hand up somebody's dress.

"I thought you were going to dump that guy, Court. He's such a loser." Even putting his reputation aside— and that was almost too generous—Nicole had caught him cheating red-handed. He had admitted as much to Courtney. Court had been pretty upset at the time, despite the fact that she was supposedly only using Kyle to make Jeff jealous. But Jeff *wasn't* jealous; he was totally in love with Hope. The whole thing made Nicole's head ache.

"Maybe I am, and maybe I'm not," Courtney said mysteriously. "I'm starting to think I might keep him around."

Nicole wheeled to face her, horrified. "What for?"

"Well . . . he *is* devastatingly handsome," Courtney said, slamming Nicole's locker shut and pushing her toward an exit door.

Nicole dragged her feet down the hall. "He's a sleaze."

"*And* he's the best kisser I ever met," Courtney continued, unperturbed.

"He's had a lot of practice. A *lot* of practice, Courtney."

"I like the way people notice when we walk into a room."

"Do you like what they say when you leave it?"

Courtney cocked one plucked brow. "What do they say?"

"If you don't know, I'm not going to tell you," Nicole said sulkily. She hated what hanging out with Kyle was doing to her friend's reputation—and to her own by association. "But if you ever want to go out with anyone nice again, you ought to get rid of Kyle right now and hope people forget about it over the summer."

"People are sheep," Courtney declared. "They'll think what I tell them to think. And I'm thinking of telling them that Kyle and I are madly in love."

Nicole dug in her heels at the door. "What? *Why?*"

Courtney only grinned. "Because stranger things have happened. I think I'm starting to fall for the guy."

"How about this one?" Leah asked, walking out of the dressing room and twirling around for Miguel's inspection.

"That looks nice," he said noncommittally.

45

She stopped in midtwirl. "You don't like it. I thought you'd like this one!"

"I do." But he was slouching in the department store chair exactly as if she *weren't* wearing a low-cut, skintight, half-see-through dress.

"Well, I'm not wearing something this daring unless you really love it. For as much of a reaction as I just got, I might as well wear the brown one."

"The brown one's nice too."

"The *brown* one?" The brown one made her look like a tall Tootsie Roll.

With a sigh, Leah dropped into the chair next to Miguel's. She had thought letting him pick out her prom dress might help cheer him up, but she was obviously fighting a losing battle. He hadn't smiled once all night. Half the time she wasn't even sure he knew where he was.

"What's the matter?" she asked, putting one of her hands over his. "Are you feeling okay?"

The astonished look he gave her made it clear she'd just said the worst possible thing.

"I mean, I know you're upset," she amended quickly. "But are you sick?"

He shook his head.

"Look, Miguel," she said impulsively. "If you don't want to go to the prom, we don't have to. I know you're sad about Zach, and if you don't think you'll have any fun there, I don't want to force you."

His brown eyes seemed to focus a little, as if she'd woken him out of a dream. "Don't you want to go?"

"Well, sure. Of course." After all, this was senior year, and their one and only chance. "But if *you* don't want—"

"I want to," he said, to her enormous relief. "I want to take you."

"Really?"

"Definitely." He flipped his hand over and gave hers a squeeze. "I'm sorry I'm such dead weight."

"Don't be sorry," she whispered, leaning closer. Her lips skimmed along his cheek, exploring the line of his jaw. Then he turned his mouth to hers and their lips met in a long, tender kiss.

"Hey! Did you know I can see right through that dress?" he broke off to demand.

Leah laughed. "Yeah. *I* know. Glad you figured it out."

Miguel made a face. "I don't like that one. And not the brown one, either. Why didn't you try on that silver one?" he asked, pointing to a mannequin across the room.

"It's kind of disco, isn't it? It looks like a floor-length mirror ball."

"I like it," he said stubbornly.

"Then I'll try it on. By all means. Don't go anywhere," she added.

Rising from her chair, Leah found a silver dress in

her size and returned to the dressing room. *Maybe it will look better on me*, she thought hopefully. Or, better still, there were other, less aggressive, silver dresses, if Miguel was suddenly into silver. But the truth was she didn't much care what she wore if it made him happier.

I should tell him I'm still sad about Zach too. She did want to go to the prom, but she didn't want Miguel to think she was heartless. If staying home would have helped Zach somehow, she'd have done it in a second.

But Zach's gone, and we have to accept it, she thought, easing scratchy sequins up her thighs. *It's terrible, but we can't all die with him. People have to get on with their lives.*

She pulled the zipper up to its stop and pushed her dressing room door open, only to find Miguel slouched down to the very edge of his chair, his gaze off in space again.

Don't they?

Four

"Let's just make a schedule and then tell people what it is," Jenna said impatiently, fishing her Eight Prime steno pad from her backpack. She had made a point of bringing it to school that Thursday, knowing she'd be taking notes about the Junior Explorers day camp. "That will be easiest."

"Yes, but I'm not sure it's such a good idea." Peter took one last bite from his sandwich, then threw the crusts into his bag. "People are really busy now, and if we set things up without asking, half of them may not be able to make it. Not to mention that we don't even have an instructor yet."

"This is the worst possible timing," Jenna complained, putting her notepad down. "I wish we could wait until summer."

"If we do, we won't be able to open the camp right when school gets out. It will mess up everything."

Jenna sighed. "I know."

The afternoon before, Peter had received a call from the Clearwater Crossing Parks Department, the agency under which he ran the Junior Explorers program. Since the day camp was peripherally connected to the park, everyone who wanted to be a counselor would have to hold water safety, first aid, and CPR certifications. Peter and Chris already had first aid and CPR, but not water safety. And since everyone in Eight Prime was planning to work with the kids at least part of the summer, they would all have to take the required classes.

"The real problem," Peter mused, "is going to be finding an instructor who's willing to work with us for free; otherwise we'll need a fund-raiser just for this. Hopefully someone will help us out, but that person's going to call the shots as far as the schedule goes."

"This is giving me a headache," Jenna said. They had already spent half of lunch trying to figure out a plan. "If we go by Eight Prime's schedule, we may not be able to get an instructor to meet it. And if we go by the instructor's schedule, Eight Prime may not be free. It's the chicken and the egg. We just have to pick a time," she insisted.

"What we *could* do is go ask everyone what nights and weekends they're free. Then, when we find an instructor, maybe we'll get lucky and everything will line up."

"You mean, like the planets?" Jenna said skeptically. Even so, it was the best idea she'd heard so far.

Gathering up the remains of her lunch, she crushed her trash into a ball and tossed it toward the can. "Two points!" she announced happily.

Peter cleared his stuff away too, and together they set off to find the other members of Eight Prime.

Ben and his friend Mark Foster were eating on a bench at the edge of the quad. Peter explained their mission while Jenna flipped to a clean page in her steno pad.

"So what nights are you free?" she asked Ben when Peter had finished. "And what about weekends?"

"I can't do anything *this* weekend," Ben reported proudly. "I'm going to the prom."

"You are?" Jenna's voice sounded a little too amazed, even to her. "I mean, you are! That's great, Ben. Who are you going with?"

"Some chick he met during all those hours he spends hanging around Angela Maldonado's locker," Mark said, rolling his eyes.

"Her name is Cheryl Churchill, she *happens* to have a locker near Angela's, and *she* happens to have asked *me*," Ben said, unperturbed. "Some people are just jealous," he added for Mark's benefit.

"That's great, Ben," Peter said. "I think everyone else is probably pretty busy with the prom this week too. But how about next week?"

"My uncle Jerry is coming over Tuesday . . . and are we having an Eight Prime meeting Thursday?"

"I hadn't planned on it," Peter said, looking at Jenna. "Do you think we should?"

"It might be easier than running around trying to catch everyone this way," she answered. "Especially with people so focused on the prom right now. If you want to, we can have it at my house."

"Okay, so then I'm busy Tuesday *and* Thursday," Ben said.

"But you're going to be with us on Thursday," said Jenna.

"Write it down," Ben insisted, pointing to her pad. The bell rang, sparing her the trouble. "I'll get everyone's schedule next Thursday," she promised as she and Peter walked off to class.

"I'll probably have more stuff on mine by then," Ben called after them.

"He acts like it's a contest," Jenna laughed to Peter.

"He just doesn't want to look like a wallflower."

"He's not a wallflower. He's going to the prom—and he's only a sophomore!"

Peter chuckled. "Our little Ben is growing up."

"Ow!" Jesse shouted, dropping his putty knife to pull a dagger of ancient paint from beneath his fingernail. Blood welled up to fill the gap, and Jesse cursed at the sight. "I should have gotten a tetanus shot before I started this."

He was well into his second afternoon of "painting" Charlie's house, and he hadn't even wet a brush yet. The exterior of the old building was entirely composed of crumbly, peeling wood, and even though Jesse kept telling himself not to worry about making things perfect, there was no way paint would stick to such a flaky surface. For the last two days he had been spraying the front of the house with a hose turned up full blast, then knocking the more stubborn areas off with a putty knife. He hadn't even looked around the back yet, and he wasn't sure he wanted to.

Why did I ever agree to do this? he wondered. A shake of his injured hand sent a drop of blood the long distance from the top of his ladder to the ground. *There have to be better ways to forget about Melanie.*

But ever since he'd given up drinking, he couldn't think of any.

What does she see in that loser Steve anyway? And why does she always go for those timid, sensitive types? I'm sensitive. I'm just not a dweeb. Can't she tell the difference?

Ignoring the blood running down his finger, Jesse picked up a second putty knife and began savagely scraping the siding.

The most irritating part was that he could have gone to the prom with practically anyone else at school. And now he wasn't even going. All that drama with Melanie had left a bad taste in his mouth, and the idea of seeing her there with Steve was too annoying to contemplate. Not that he was jealous. Far from it. It was more like he was fed up.

Besides, who cares about a stupid prom anyway? If it's such a big deal, I can always go next year.

Which is why when Robin Conner had asked him at lunch that day, he had turned her down flat. He barely knew her anyway, except for seeing her in homeroom. She was pretty cute, though, and if she had asked him before that mess with Melanie, he might at least have considered her. But Robin wasn't popular, and to say yes to her now, when everyone cool was already hooked up, could have really hurt his rep. Better not to show up at all than risk a hint of desperation. Besides, he could always make up a decent excuse for not going to the dance; it was much harder to come up with one for not already having a date.

Whatever, he thought impatiently, trying to put Melanie and the prom out of his mind as his hand scraped back and forth, knocking splintered paint from splintered wood. The morning weather had been sunny and clear, but now the sky had turned gray and the air oppressively humid—signs an uprooted Californian was finally learning to recognize as foretelling thundershowers.

It would be just my luck to get hit by lightning, Jesse thought, glancing nervously at the horizon. *Up here on a metal ladder, with a metal scraper in my hand . . . I might as well go up on the roof and wave a golf club around.*

He tried to imagine how much it would hurt to be hit by lightning. Probably it wouldn't turn him into a genius, like in the movies, either. At least he didn't wear jewelry, though, because he had once seen a TV story about lightning-strike victims who'd had the shapes of their jewelry burnt into their flesh like strange black tattoos. He remembered one man in particular, who had been wearing a large silver cross. The bolt had hit the cross directly, burning its outline onto his chest, even including the chain.

Wearing a mark like that every day would have to make a guy think. Jesse glanced at the sky again, not ready for anything so intense.

He had just about finished scraping what he could reach without moving the ladder when the sound of the front door opening made him freeze. Charlie was coming out onto the porch, the metal legs of his walker screeching across the old boards.

"Whatcha doing up there?" he called, leaning over the railing to peer up at Jesse.

Jesse groaned. "Tap dancing. What's it look like?"

"You haven't started painting yet?"

"Well, excuse me, but there's a couple hundred years' worth of scum on these boards. Putting paint on top of that would be totally pointless."

"What you want to do is knock that loose stuff off with the hose, like I said."

"I already tried the hose, Charlie. There's not that much water pressure in all of Missouri."

"Did you use that good spray nozzle? You have to—"

"Do you want to do this yourself?" Jesse snapped. "I don't see you up on this ladder."

It was a low blow, considering that the old guy could barely drag himself around even with a walker, but Jesse wasn't in the best possible mood.

"I forgot you already know every—" Charlie began snidely.

"Look, Charlie, I can do this job, or I can listen to you. But I'm not doing both. The house is getting painted my way or not at all."

Charlie started to say something, then shook his head. "Fine. Heaven forbid I should try to help you."

Turning his walker around seemed to take the old guy a hundred years. Jesse practically held his breath until Charlie disappeared back into the house, and then he sighed with relief. It wasn't that he didn't *like* Charlie—he just didn't want anyone telling him what to do. Especially not right then.

Besides, he knew I was a pain in the butt when he hired me. What does he expect for a hundred bucks?

"I'll do it," Nicole decided, reaching for the phone lying beside her on the bed.

A second later, her hand came back empty. She just couldn't make up her mind whether or not to ask Guy to the prom.

First of all, there was that whole big argument they'd had over her trying out for the cheerleading squad.

Well, maybe it was more of a disagreement.

Either way, it still rankled that he'd called cheerleading shallow. And if he even *thought* about pretending she was better off not making the squad . . .

On the other hand, it *was* kind of a relief to know that her not being a cheerleader wouldn't be a disappointment to him. It was enough of a disappointment to her. She could still barely walk down the hall at school without feeling like everyone was looking at her. The only thing that could have been worse was not having made Sandra's list at all.

If I have to be a loser, at least I'm the number-one loser. Wait, that didn't sound very good. I mean, at least I'm the runner-up.

She still had no illusions about actually getting onto the squad, but perhaps there was a little more dignity in being the runner-up than she had initially realized. A couple of people had actually congratulated her on it.

Maybe I ought to hold my head up, like Melanie said. And going to the prom with Guy is better than not going

57

at all. *Why stay home and look like even more of a loser than I am?*

Nicole reached for the phone again.

Except what if he says no?

Would he?

Her hand drew back, hesitated, then grabbed the telephone. She would never know unless she asked, and it wasn't as if she had a lot of other potential dates lined up.

It wasn't as if she had *one*.

If he says no, then I'll know things are over between us, Nicole thought as she dialed. *This is good, actually. A push like this might be just what we need.*

Although she couldn't help remembering the last time she'd tried to push things along, by kissing Guy at the bowling alley. She'd never been more embarrassed than when he'd told her he wasn't ready to take things to that level. *Whatever that—*

"Hello?" Guy's familiar voice answered.

"Hi, it's Nicole," she said quickly, before she could chicken out. Her voice sounded a little breathless, but she rushed ahead anyway. "What are you doing?"

"Not much. I was wondering if I was ever going to hear from you again."

What's that supposed to mean? she thought. It hadn't been *that* long since their date at the ice skating rink, and it wasn't as if she had heard from him, either. Or had he picked up on the fact that she hadn't been too happy with him then? The possibility made her even more nervous than she already was.

"Jeff told me you didn't make cheerleader," he said, breaking into the silence. "I'm sorry."

"You are?"

"Well, sure. I mean, I know you wanted it."

"Um, yeah. Thanks," she squeaked, choked up. She hadn't expected him to care.

"You got runner-up, though, right? That's still pretty good."

"Runner-up's just a formality," she managed somehow. "It doesn't mean anything."

"You never know," he said.

"I guess."

"So. You guys have a prom this weekend. Jeff's taking Hope, so I've been hearing things."

"Oh. Right." She'd been hoping to bring up the prom her own way.

"Are you going with anyone?"

Nicole cringed. She had *really* been hoping to bring up that part her own way.

"Well, not yet. I, uh—"

"Can I take you?" he asked abruptly. "I just . . . I guess I would understand if you wanted to go with someone from your own school, but I was hoping—"

"All right," she said quickly.

"Yeah? You mean it?"

"I wasn't even sure if I wanted to go," she said, trying to sound blasé. "But if *you* want to . . ."

"What time should I pick you up?" Guy asked. "Do you want to double with Hope and Jeff, or should we go on our own?"

"On our own. Definitely." Nicole sat up on her bed. "Are we going out to dinner first?"

"Sure. Where do you want to go?"

"Where do *you* want to go?"

They hashed out the details of their evening right down to Nicole's corsage, and when she finally hung up the phone she was more excited than she'd have thought possible.

"Mom!" she shouted, bursting out of her bedroom and barreling down the stairs. "Mom, I need a new dress!"

Mrs. Brewster was in the dining room, waxing the long dining table. "What kind of dress?" she asked.

"Something hot. That looks good with white rosebuds. I'm going to the prom!"

Her mother straightened up, the rag dangling forgotten in her hand. "With who?"

"Guy Vaughn. He just asked me."

"Congratulations. But I'm afraid new formals aren't in the budget right now, especially since you still have that red one I bought you for Homecoming that you never even wore."

60

"I wore it!" Nicole protested. "I wore it in L.A. when I went to the U. S. Girls contest."

"Well, for what that thing cost you can wear it twice. At least."

"Mommm," she started to whine, but a sharp glance from Mrs. Brewster stopped her on the spot. "Oh, all right."

After all, Guy hadn't even discovered she was in Los Angeles until after she'd worn the dress, so he definitely hadn't seen it. No one she knew had, except the three other girls in Eight Prime, and they weren't going to care—if they even remembered.

And it *was* hot. And it went with white roses.

Nicole turned and ran back up the stairs, already getting used to the idea. The dress was at one end of her closet, still in a plastic sheath from the dry cleaners. She ripped it free and rushed to the full-length mirror on her bathroom door, holding the fabric up against her body.

My black heels, she mused, mentally adding them to her reflection. *And my black crystal necklace and earrings . . . How should I wear my hair?*

She draped her dress over the back of her desk chair and started digging through the unmade blankets on her bed for her latest *New Look* magazine. There was a style she'd just seen that might be perfect.

Yes! That ought to turn a few heads, she thought, smiling as she found the page. *I think I'll try it out now.*

Magazine in hand, she ran into the bathroom, genuinely excited. Maybe having some pride, like Melanie said, wouldn't get her on the squad, but it might at least stop people from talking trash about her.

"Besides," she told her reflection, her grin growing by the second. "It's the *prom*!"

Five

I ought to get Miguel to help me, Jesse thought grouchily, walking out into CCHS's central quad amid the rest of the lunchtime crowd. *He used to have a job painting buildings. He ought to be pretty good at it by now.*

But Jesse had heard about Zach from Peter, so he knew Miguel was hurting. It didn't seem like the best possible time to ask him for a favor.

Not everyone drowns their sorrows in paint fumes.

Even so, he had to have some help. The way things were going, he'd have to leave for college before he finished half of Charlie's house.

Stopping at the edge of the concrete, Jesse scanned the quad, searching for potential victims. For a moment, he almost considered asking some guys from the football team, but the link between Charlie and Coach Davis was too sensitive, and Jesse didn't want to take a chance on having that story get around.

No, Miguel is the perfect person, he thought, still scanning. *I'll bet Miguel wouldn't talk under torture.*

Or what about Peter?

63

Now that Jesse thought about it, this type of do-good project was right up Peter's alley, and after all the charity stuff Jesse had helped him with, he could hardly say no. Maybe Peter wasn't as strong or as experienced as Miguel—but he'd be a whole lot better than nothing.

Jesse's gaze sought out the quadside table where Peter and Jenna had resumed eating now that the weather had warmed. Sure enough, they were there again that Friday, along with Ben and that blond kid he was always hanging around with. Jesse grimaced at the sight of Ben, but he didn't hesitate before he started walking.

"Hey. How's it going?" he said, dropping into the empty seat beside Peter. "What's for lunch today?"

"Spaghetti Surprise," Ben reported, pointing to his tray with his fork. "Not bad!"

"What's the surprise?" Jesse asked dubiously, eyeing the saucy red cube. "That people are actually eating it?"

"I think it's that they crammed it into pans and then cut it up like lasagna," Ben said. "It tastes like spaghetti, though."

"Like school spaghetti, you mean," his friend corrected him.

"Right," said Ben. "They ought to call it *School* Spaghetti Surprise. Or, wait! I Can't Believe It's Not Spaghetti!"

"I can believe it," Jesse muttered. "I think I'll check out the vending machines."

Jenna wrinkled her nose but kept eating. "It's not as bad as their fish sticks."

"I'm definitely buying chips now," he said.

"Go and get them. We'll save your seat," Ben offered.

"Nah, that's all right. I just want to ask Peter something."

Peter put down his sandwich. "What?" he asked curiously.

"There's this old guy I know, Charlie. I helped him out with some chores around his house back in November."

Peter nodded. "Yeah. I remember."

"Anyway, he practically begged me to paint his house for him. The place is a disaster—I'd rather walk to the North Pole barefoot. But he's old and alone . . . so I said I would. He's paying me a hundred bucks, but that's mostly for his pride. He couldn't begin to afford what the job is worth."

"Then it's nice of you to help him out," Peter said.

"Yeah, well. About that . . ." Jesse didn't pause long enough to let himself feel guilty for asking. "It's turning into an even bigger job than I realized, and I was wondering if you could help me. I'll split the money with you—what there is of it."

"Me? Sure." If Peter was unhappy about being

drafted, he didn't let it show. "When do you want me to be there?"

"How about Saturday? I've been working the last two afternoons, so I'm taking this one off. But if we get an early start Saturday, we should get a lot done."

"I'll be there as early as I can, but I have Junior Explorers in the morning. It will probably be more like noon."

"I can be there early!" Ben piped in eagerly.

Jesse stifled a groan. Knowing Ben, he'd spill the paint, walk through it, and track up the whole neighborhood. The only way he was likely to get any on the walls was if he spilled it on himself first, then fell against the house.

"Do you want to start at eight?" Ben persisted.

On the other hand, there was a whole lot of scraping still to be done. As long as Ben stayed off the ladder, he ought to be pretty safe with a putty knife.

"Make it nine," Jesse said. "I don't want to wake up the whole neighborhood."

He drew a map to Charlie's house on a napkin, then stood up to leave. "I'm going to get some lunch. I'll see you guys Saturday."

He hurried off before anyone could change his mind—or before Ben could offer to save his seat again. He wasn't feeling that sociable to begin with, so he really didn't want to hang out with Ben. He began walking toward the cafeteria, thinking of joining the football team, then abruptly changed direction. He didn't want to risk an encounter with Melanie if she was sitting with the cheerleaders.

Or with that jerk Steve Carson.

Just remembering the way she'd paraded Carson in front of him in the parking lot on Wednesday made his chest feel tight. She'd tried to make it look like Carson had shown up accidentally, but Jesse hadn't been fooled—once she had them all together, she couldn't wait to mention the prom. And what was she doing in the gym parking lot anyway? What kind of game was she playing?

More to the point, why do you care?

I don't, he thought savagely. *She can do whatever she wants.*

Changing direction yet again, he headed toward the library. A green and gold banner over its entrance hyped the prom, putting him in an even worse mood. He slunk under it, hoping for a dark, quiet corner to sulk in.

The sooner the stupid prom is over, the better. Melanie can't be planning to keep Steve around after the dance.

Can she?

"What are you doing tonight, *mi hijo?*" Mrs. del Rios asked Miguel over dinner. "Are you and Leah going out?"

"Not tonight," he said listlessly, pushing bites of chicken around his plate. "The prom's tomorrow, so we didn't make plans tonight."

"I wish they had a prom at Sacred Heart," Rosa said, getting a dreamy look in her dark eyes. "That's the only thing I feel like I'm missing by going to Catholic school."

"They have dances. They have that big formal with St. Xavier's," Mrs. del Rios said, naming an all-boys school in Red River.

"Yeah, but it's not the same," Rosa said. "It's not a *prom*."

"I don't know what you think a prom is." Putting down his fork, Miguel pushed his plate away. "It's just a regular dance, except that people waste lots more money renting clothes and limousines."

"Oh, that's nice," Rosa said indignantly. The color rose in her olive cheeks, pink against black hair and brows. "Leah's a lucky girl to be going with such a romantic."

Miguel rose wearily from the table. "It's Rosa's turn to do the dishes," he told his mother. "I'm going to my room."

"Are you sick, *mi vida?*" she asked, concerned. "You barely ate tonight."

She didn't mention Zach's name, but he could tell she knew what was really bothering him.

"I'm just tired."

In his room, with the door shut behind him, Mi-

68

guel didn't even turn on the light. There was nothing he needed to see. He fell backward across his neatly made bed, with his feet hanging over the edge, his shoes making dull thuds as he kicked them off one by one.

Peace at last, he thought, closing his eyes. *Or quiet, anyway*.

He welcomed the chance to be alone. Eight days had passed since Zach's death, but Miguel barely knew what to make of them. His pain was still as raw, as fresh as if the tragedy had just happened—except that it felt like he'd been sad forever.

At school, the people who didn't know about Zach went on as if nothing had happened, and the ones who did pussyfooted around him. Miguel wasn't sure which was worse—or even what he expected. He just wanted to stop feeling out of step with the whole world, as if he were the only one who truly understood how bad things were.

In the bottom drawer of his dresser, squashed flat under his jeans, was the bag Mrs. Dewey had sent him via Howard. He still hadn't opened it, and he didn't think he ever would. He couldn't even imagine how Mrs. Dewey had found the strength to put it together after losing her only child. But knowing there was someone hurting more than he didn't make Miguel hurt less—or feel any more cheerful. To return to his normal life, to ever feel happy again, just didn't seem fair to Zach. All Miguel could do for

Zach now was remember, and he planned to do that for the rest of his life.

I ought to go to his grave, Miguel thought, wishing once again that he'd been invited to the funeral. Nothing felt final the way it was. Zach was buried, but not to him.

How would I find it, though?

Leah had told him that in Jewish tradition the tombstone was usually erected a year after burial. Did that mean there was no marker at all there now? Or maybe one of those anonymous little plates with numbers on it? How would he know which grave was Zach's?

It will be the fresh one, he realized. *The one where the cuts still show in the grass.*

The thought made him abandon the whole idea. He didn't want to see that.

I just wish I could have said good-bye. Things felt so wrong, the way they had ended.

"Zach, are you up there, bud?" he whispered. "I miss you."

I really miss you a lot.

"This'll do," Melanie murmured, checking her reflection in the three-way dressing room mirror. The knee-length black chiffon was only the second dress she'd tried on, but it was good enough. If she'd cared about perfection, she wouldn't have waited until the night before the prom to go shopping.

70

Now if I were going with Jesse . . . Well, that would be different.

She still didn't understand exactly what had happened when she'd tried to talk to him on Wednesday. All she knew for sure was that he'd made her so mad she'd been happy for the chance to flaunt her date with Steve. An hour later, though, when the adrenaline had worn off, she'd felt even worse than before.

If only I knew what was in his mind when he asked me!

Had his offer meant anything? Or did he just need a date?

After all, I did go out of my way to let him know I was available. As he so gentlemanly pointed out.

Not that she really believed he'd asked her out of pity.

But then why did he ask me? She'd been racking her brain for a week and she still didn't have the slightest idea.

Reaching behind her, she unzipped the black dress and slipped its spaghetti straps off her shoulders. Her father had loaned her his credit card that evening, and had even given her a ride to the mall. A bus home was due in fifteen minutes, though, and if she could catch it without having to make him come get her, they would probably both be happier.

"Going to the prom?" the lady behind the counter asked as she rang up the dress. "Who's the lucky guy?"

71

"Just a friend," Melanie said, pitching her tone to discourage conversation. She glanced at her wristwatch as well, reinforcing her point.

But the woman seemed oblivious. "You never know," she said, smiling. "Plenty of romances start out as friendships."

"Uh-huh," Melanie replied, forcing a weak smile of her own. But inside she was thinking of Jesse. And she wasn't smiling at all.

Who would he be with at the prom? Would it be someone she knew? Would she be able to convince him she didn't care?

Just thinking about it was killing her.

"Here you go. Have a wonderful time," the woman said, handing over the dress at last. She had wrapped it in tissue paper and put it in the bottom of a fancy shopping bag with string handles. Melanie had to force herself not to snatch the bag away in her desire to run for the door.

Just focus on Steve, she advised herself as she hurried out of the store. *Steve's nice, and cute, and sweet.*

And simple.

Her eyes burned with unshed tears as the automatic doors whirred open to let her into the parking lot. She took big gulps of the fresh night air, forcing it into her aching lungs.

You have to get a grip on yourself. If you can't even think about Jesse without crying, how are you going to be in a room with him and his date without making a scene?

That question was the final straw. A hot, fat tear slid down Melanie's cheek as she threaded through the parked cars. Luckily, no one else was waiting at the bus stop. Finding a tissue in her backpack, she wiped her eyes and blew her nose.

You have to stop this, she told herself. *Thinking about Jesse is just more pain than gain.*

Six

"How about this?" Courtney asked, holding a huge silk magnolia against her red curls. "What if I wore my hair up, with this on the side?"

"It's kind of big," said Nicole.

"True. I wonder if they have a smaller one."

Courtney began digging through the buckets of silk flowers outside a gift shop door while Nicole tapped an impatient foot. They had come to the mall that Saturday morning to pick up the guys' boutonnieres and do a little last-minute shopping, but Nicole wanted to look at nail polish and all Courtney could think about was her hair.

"You're already going to have a corsage," Nicole reminded her, desperate to get moving. "There's probably such a thing as too many flowers."

Courtney straightened up. "What are you wearing in your hair?"

"Just . . . a thing."

"What kind of thing?"

"It's . . . kind of a black crystal headband."

If she used the word *tiara*, Court would be sure to get the wrong idea, and Nicole wasn't up for the public abuse. She knew she wasn't going to be prom queen—but did that mean she couldn't look good? Besides, the way she was going to pile her hair up behind it, it really *was* more like a headband. Sort of a *vertical* headband.

"Maybe *I* should get a headband," Courtney mused.

"Good idea! You know where they have a lot of those? Next to makeup counters. Let's go." Grabbing Courtney by a sleeve, Nicole began pulling her toward the department store at the end of the mall.

"Geez, what's your hurry?" Courtney complained. "I thought we were going to have some fun."

"We are. Tonight. But I've got a million things to do before then. I've got to wash my hair and shave my legs and paint my fingernails and toes. Then I've got to set my hair and do my makeup and—"

Nicole broke off her litany to check her watch, not a bit reassured by the fact that it was barely noon. "It's going to be touch and go already. Come *on*, Court. Hurry up!"

"You worry too much," Courtney said. "Relax."

Like the whole world is going to stop turning just because you say so. Nicole had to bite her lip to keep from saying it out loud. Knowing Courtney, she probably thought it should. But while she was busy relaxing, Nicole was losing precious time.

I should have come by myself, she thought. *It would have been such an easy thing to get in, get my stuff, and get out. Why didn't I?*

Maybe because she knew shopping together would be her only chance that day to spend time with her best friend. Once she and Courtney got to the dance, they wouldn't be hanging out much. Not when Court was going to be there with Kyle—and Jeff was going to be there with Hope. Nicole wasn't sure if she felt guilty about that or if she was just afraid of what might happen, but every time she thought about Courtney and Hope at the same prom, her stomach started going through the spin cycle.

"Court, there's something I think you should know," she blurted out, feeling like she had to say it. "Jeff *is* bringing Hope to the prom. I mean, that's definitely happening."

"So?"

"So, are you okay with that? I mean . . ."

"I'm not going to make a scene, if that's what you're worried about," Courtney said haughtily.

That was *exactly* what she was worried about. "I just meant—"

"I don't know why you even think I care anymore. I'm tired of Jeff and his little games."

"You are?"

"Of course! What is he thinking, anyway, trying to make me jealous with someone who looks just like me? He's such a boy. At least Kyle is a man."

76

Is that what you call him? But once again Nicole kept the comment to herself. Courtney had already promised not to make a scene at the prom, and that was the main thing.

"You know what you ought to wear in your hair?" Nicole said, feeling generous all of a sudden. "A feather. A green feather to match your dress."

"A feather?" Courtney repeated dubiously.

"Yeah. Kind of swooping over the top. Like this." Nicole piled her hair on top of her head and tried to pat it into the mound Courtney's curls would make. With her free hand, she gestured diagonally from back to front, indicating the feather.

Courtney's eyes narrowed speculatively. "I don't know. I've never seen anything like that."

"English debutantes used to wear feathers when they were presented to the queen. White ones. I saw it in a book."

"Really? But where are we going to find a green feather?"

Good question. Nicole couldn't think of anyplace in the mall, and a drive downtown would really eat into her prom preparation time. On the other hand, she'd been the genius with the suggestion. She couldn't very well tell Court to forget it now.

"The costume shop on Main Street?" she ventured at last. "Maybe they can take it out of a boa or something."

"All right," Courtney said, clearly warming to

the idea. "Let's go." She stopped walking and turned around right at the entrance to the department store.

"I just need to get some nail polish first," Nicole said, starting to make a dash for the makeup counter.

But Courtney was faster. "Ni-*cole*!" she scolded, grabbing her by one wrist. "I thought we were in a hurry! You must have nail polish at home."

"I don't! Not the kind—"

"Well, you know they don't have feathers in there, and you can get polish anywhere. In fact, they probably have some at the costume shop. Let's go."

Courtney started marching toward the mall exit, pulling Nicole reluctantly behind her. Nicole knew exactly what she wanted, and it wasn't some ugly, cheap brand she'd never heard of.

"Courtney, I just—"

"Don't be so selfish, Nicole! Do you know how late it is? How am I ever going to get my hair done in time if you keep dragging your feet? We have to leave right now."

Nicole could barely believe her ears. Part of her felt like telling Courtney to go get her own feather. Another, less inhibited, part even felt like telling her where to stick it. She was sick and tired of kissing up to Courtney, always putting her needs first. . . .

But it wouldn't be worth it—fighting with Courtney never was. Court could carry a grudge much longer than Nicole could stay mad, which meant she was the one who always ended up suffering more, no matter who had been right.

"All right, fine," she said irritably, abandoning her dream of iridescent designer polish. "Red is red. I guess."

"Now you're talking sense. Finally." Courtney rolled her bottle green eyes. "Honestly, Nicole. Sometimes I think the only person you care about is yourself."

"I can't believe we're actually ready to paint," Jesse told Peter, surveying Charlie's house from the sidewalk. The place looked worse than ever after so much scraping—half old yellowed paint and half dingy gray wood—but the front and side walls were finally smooth enough.

"I wish we could have finished prepping the back wall, too," Peter said, glancing at the falling sun. "Maybe tomorrow, but I'll have to see."

Jesse checked his watch. "Why not now? We still have a couple hours of daylight."

But Peter shook his head. "Not really. I'm taking Jenna to dinner early, and I have to get home and clean up first. I don't think she'd be too happy if I showed up looking like this." Like Jesse, he was covered in dirt and paint shavings, a layer of fine white dust clinging to his hair and eyelashes like a coating of talcum powder.

"That's all right," Jesse said grudgingly. "At least Ben can stay and help me." Ben had turned out to be surprisingly useful, actually, his only big mistake being leaving the lid open on the pizza box and then scraping paint directly above it. Luckily, they were all mostly full by then.

As if he had heard his name, Ben chose that moment to come out from behind the house, his sopping wet shirt dripping onto his shoes. His hair was wet as well, making it even more limp than usual.

"What happened to you?" Jesse demanded.

"The back of the house is sprayed down," Ben reported sheepishly. "Then I dropped the hose on the sprayer handle, and the thing went off by itself."

"You look like you took a swim," Peter said, laughing. "Did you bring any extra clothes?"

"No, but I have to go now anyway. Big date tonight, you know."

Ben smiled in spite of his recent soaking, but Jesse couldn't share his joy. He still couldn't get over the fact that Ben was going to the prom. Ben! There was just something wrong about that—especially when Jesse was staying home.

"Do you want us to help you pick up these tools?" Peter asked. "Or are you going to be here awhile?"

"Huh? Oh." Jesse tried to focus on the matter at hand. "I'll take care of it."

"Okay, I'm going to run, then," said Ben, shivering

in the afternoon shadows. "If I can, I'll come by here tomorrow, but I think my parents have something planned."

"Whatever," Jesse said.

Peter had brushed most of the loose grime off his clothes and was edging toward the curb as well. "Have fun at your concert tonight," he told Jesse.

"Huh? Oh. Right."

That was the official lie—the one Jesse had made up to cover his absence from the prom: He was driving to Springfield to see Concrete Bullet that night, along with a supposed date from Mapleton. He didn't even like the band that much, but he'd seen in the paper that they were playing, and they were popular enough to provide an acceptable excuse—especially since he wasn't actually going. He was counting on the fact that no one else from CCHS would be going either, and therefore he couldn't be caught in his lie.

How could *anyone be going, when they'll all be at the prom?* he thought sullenly as Peter and Ben drove off in separate cars. He was starting to think he was the only teenager in all of Clearwater Crossing who wouldn't be there. Had he made a mistake by not asking someone else after Melanie? He could still probably get a date—even now.

The problem was, he didn't want to go with anyone else—even now.

"I'm just going to clean this stuff up and leave," he muttered, kicking at the hose sprawled all over the lawn. There might be daylight left, but suddenly he didn't feel like working.

He didn't feel like going to the prom.

And he sure didn't feel like going home.

I feel like getting drunk.

It would be easy that night, too. There were going to be after-prom parties all over town. He knew of at least two keggers, no invitation required. All he'd have to do was show up. If he got there late enough, he could even maintain his cover story about the concert.

Collapsing the ladder, Jesse threw it under the front porch. A minute later, the rest of the tools followed. He left the hose where it was, too disgusted to bother coiling it up. He didn't even tell Charlie he was leaving before he climbed into his BMW and roared off down the street, revving the powerful engine.

Whether he wanted to or not, he had to go home, because he had to take a shower. But after that . . .

He could tell his dad and Elsa anything. They never checked. He could stay out all night if he wanted to. Jesse had promised Coach Davis, his stepsister, Brittany, and probably a few other people that he wouldn't touch liquor again until he was twenty-one. But so long as he didn't get caught . . .

He imagined Melanie slow dancing with Steve Carson—her arms around his neck, his hands sliding down to her waist—and the pain in his gut made him gasp.

"I want to," he decided.

"You look . . . gorgeous," Peter breathed, his eyes wide with admiration. "Wow!"

Jenna giggled self-consciously. "So do you," she returned, opening her front door wider.

"Are you ready to go?" he asked.

"No, we have to get a picture first," Mrs. Conrad said from the entryway. "Come on in, Peter. I want you two to pose by the fireplace." The camera dangled from a strap around her neck as she shepherded Jenna and Peter into the living room, where the rest of the Conrads were waiting.

"Peter! Nice penguin suit," Mr. Conrad teased. "Very stylish."

Peter smiled down at his rented black tuxedo. "Do you like it? I'm thinking of becoming a conductor."

"On a train?" asked Allison, confused.

"Of an orchestra, stupid," Maggie corrected.

Caitlin shot Maggie a disapproving look.

"I don't get it," Sarah said. "I think Peter looks handsome."

"So do I," Jenna leaned closer to whisper in his ear. He smelled like freshly washed hair and a hint of aftershave. She kept leaning over until her nose grazed his cheek, sending a happy little shiver right down to her toes.

"We all do, sweetie," Mrs. Conrad assured Sarah.

"Then why did Daddy call him a penguin?"

"He was kidding. Now come on, you two," she said, looking through her camera. "Get in nice and close."

Jenna sidled nearer to Peter, the netting on her long skirt crunching between them. There would be a photographer at the prom, but she was glad her mom was taking pictures now, while her hairstyle was still intact. She was even wearing a bit of makeup—mascara and pale pink lipstick—and she wanted to capture the look before it wore off.

"Okay. Everybody say cheese," Mrs. Conrad directed, her finger flexing on the shutter.

Jenna flashed her a happy smile.

"Wait!" Mr. Conrad cried. "Don't you want them with their flowers on?"

"Oops," Peter said sheepishly. "I left your corsage in the car."

"Yours is in the refrigerator," Jenna admitted.

Everything stopped while the flowers were fetched. Jenna gasped when she saw her corsage: a wristband of tiny, blush-pink roses with accents of delicate fern.

"I hope you like it," Peter said, stretching the elastic for her to slip her hand through. "I didn't know what shade of pink your dress was."

"They're so beautiful!" she said, holding the flowers up against her bodice. "They match perfectly!"

"I got lucky," Peter mumbled, turning a little pink himself.

She had finally decided on a white rose boutonniere for him, but securing it to his lapel proved trickier than she had expected.

"Ouch! You had it easy with the elastic," she told him, jabbing the pin through the heavy layers of fabric right into her index finger. She tried again; failed again. "It might help if you stopped laughing."

She finally got the rose on right, Peter put his arm across her shoulders, and Mrs. Conrad snapped the picture. Jenna knew the moment the flash went off that it was going to be a good one. In her mind, it was already framed and on her desk. Unless the photographer at the dance took an even better one . . .

"We should get going," she said, excited to start the evening. She and Peter both had curfews, so she didn't want to waste a minute of their time together.

Caitlin stood up from her place on the couch. "Here. I got you something," she said, producing a disposable camera from behind her back. "You can take pictures of all your friends."

"Cat!" Jenna exclaimed, touched by her sister's thoughtfulness. Shy Caitlin hadn't gone to her own proms, which made the gesture doubly sweet. "Thanks," she said, crushing her sister in a hug. "You're the best."

At last Jenna and Peter made it out the door, her entire family crowding onto the doorstep to yell their final farewells.

"Have a good time!"

"Don't be late!"

"We won't," Jenna promised, waving back.

The evening air was warm on her bare shoulders, but she shivered with excitement as Peter opened the passenger door, waiting for her to gather her full skirts around her before shutting it again. He had borrowed his mother's car for the occasion, a shiny black four-door, and Jenna felt truly elegant as they pulled away from the curb.

"I still can't believe you got us a dinner reservation at the Lakehouse Lodge." All week Jenna had been hearing complaints about the restaurants at the prom site being booked solid. "You must have made it weeks ago!"

Peter smiled mysteriously. "I have my methods."

Jenna tried to settle into her seat for the long ride to the lake, but she was so excited she could barely sit still. Dinner was going to be fun, but she couldn't wait for the dance. She and Peter had been to lots of dances together as friends, but this would be their first as a couple—not to mention their first prom! She could hardly wait for the whole school to see them in each other's arms, dancing the night away.

"You know, Jenna," said Peter, breaking into her

reverie, "you really do look pretty tonight. I mean, not that you don't usually. But *tonight* . . ."

She grinned at him, her heart on fire. How could she ever tell him how much he meant to her?

"Peter?"

"Yeah?"

"Just . . . I'll tell you later."

Seven

"Wow! Look at the lights!" Steve exclaimed as their long black limo pulled up in front of the Lakehouse Lodge. White bulbs dripped like icing from every eave, column, and window ledge, giving the log façade of the big hotel a festive, romantic appearance.

"It's beautiful," Melanie said, but her voice sounded dead in her ears. "Dinner was great too," she added, forcing more enthusiasm.

Steve had picked her up right on time, looking like a model in his tuxedo, his fair hair slicked straight back. He had brought her a gorgeous single orchid corsage, and taken her to Le Papillon for dinner. He had been nothing but cute, sweet, and attentive.

So why am I so miserable?

"I'm glad you liked it," he said, leaning a little closer. Their legs came into contact, just barely touching. He hesitated, then put his hand over one of hers, leaning closer still.

Her heart began to race. Was he going to kiss her? Now? It was barely eight o'clock!

Something in her eyes must have tipped him off. He sat back abruptly, looking confused.

"Should, uh . . . should we go inside?" he asked.

"Yes! That would be great," she said, relieved.

The chauffeur came around to open their doors. Steve hurried to scramble out first and then reached in for Melanie's hand. Limos were stopped everywhere, most with four or five couples piling out, like those *Guinness Book of World Records* attempts to see how many people could stuff a phone booth. It was almost embarrassing to have one all to themselves when everyone else was sharing to cover the cost. Steve was obviously pulling out all the stops to impress her.

You could try a little harder, too, she told herself, cranking up her smile a notch as they followed the overdressed crowd into an opulent lobby.

Crystal chandeliers hung low from the ceiling, their glittering reflection bouncing off darkened windows framing the lake. Melanie could just discern the lanterned edge of a long outdoor deck, and the silhouettes of a few couples taking advantage of the moonlit view.

"This is nice," she said, slipping her hand through Steve's arm and tilting her head against his shoulder. "I can't believe I've never been here before."

Steve smiled. "The first thing we have to do is get our picture taken. I want to remember the way you look now for the rest of my life."

The sincerity of the compliment left her unsure how to reply.

"You probably say that to all the other girls too," she teased, deciding to joke it off.

Steve peered around the dazzling room as if it all lay in darkness. "What other girls?" he asked.

They had their picture taken in the booth at the entrance to the ballroom—black on black, blond on blonde. The photographer made Melanie stand on a box to bring her face closer to Steve's.

"You two are gorgeous together," she purred as she focused her camera. "What a couple. Now, smile!"

A blinding flash went off, leaving Melanie still seeing stars as they walked into the dance. Or perhaps those spots were reflections from the mirror balls overhead. Lights swirled and sparkled everywhere, filling the darkened ballroom with motion.

"What do you want to do first?" Steve asked. "We should probably find a table, because we'll never get one later. Is there anyone in particular you want to sit with?"

Around the perimeter of the large room was a host of round, white-draped tables with star-shaped balloon centerpieces. Few chairs were occupied, but the coats and purses draped over them made it clear how many had been reserved. Later, when people got tired of dancing, the tables would be packed.

"Maybe we should," Melanie said, wondering where Tanya and the other cheerleaders were sitting.

On second thought, she didn't necessarily want to hang out with the cheerleaders—not if they were hanging with the football players. She wondered where Leah and Miguel were, or Peter and Jenna, but there were so many people milling about and most of the room was so dark that there was almost no chance of spotting anyone in particular. "I don't think it really matters where."

Steve beamed, and she suddenly realized he'd been hoping not to be saddled with a bunch of people he didn't know. "By the dance floor is good," he suggested. "If we get bored we can make scorecards and do some Olympics-style judging."

Melanie laughed. "That ought to go over big."

They found a place Steve liked just as Tanya came running up solo in a cream satin dress. "Hey! I saved you seats over there," she said, pointing off into the darkness. "You have to come sit with us."

"Who's us?" Melanie asked cautiously. "I don't want to sit with Vanessa."

"Do I look crazy? Neither do I," said Tanya. "No, it's a bunch of the new squad and their dates. Everybody's cool."

Melanie felt torn. "I don't know. Do you mind?" she asked Steve, hoping he'd say he did. But he just shook his head.

"It doesn't matter to me. One place is as good as another."

They trailed Tanya through the ballroom, Melanie

picking more and more people out of the crowd. She caught a glimpse of Jenna and Peter, then spotted Ben with a quart of gel in his hair and an unknown girl on his arm.

"Here we are!" Tanya announced, pulling coats off a couple of chairs and piling them up on others. "Those are for you guys."

"Thanks." Melanie dropped her shawl onto a seat and stood looking around her. Sure enough, Barry Stein and Gary Baldwin, two of Jesse's football buddies, were at a nearby table, with two vacant chairs next to them.

"Is Jesse Jones sitting over there?" she asked abruptly.

"Why?" Tanya countered.

She seemed surprised by the question, and Steve looked puzzled too. Melanie felt herself blushing as she realized that she could have been more subtle.

"It's nothing. It's just, uh, that group we're in," she said, fumbling for a plausible excuse. "I have a message for him, that's all."

"Well, he's not sitting there, and I haven't seen him," Tanya answered. "I don't think he's here."

"No?"

Was it possible he wasn't coming? And if so, why didn't she feel more relieved at the prospect of not having to see him with another girl?

Because now I'm going to spend all night wondering where he is, she realized unhappily.

If she had simply minded her own business and not encouraged Steve, she would *know* where Jesse was now, because he'd be right there beside her. Everything would be fine.

I am such an idiot.

"Do you want to dance?" Steve asked.

The deejay had just started a popular new song. It seemed that half the school was suddenly mobbing the dance floor.

"If you do."

Steve held out his hand and Melanie slipped hers into it, trying to concentrate on him. He was handsome. He was nice. He deserved so much better than she could give him.

"Are you sure you want to do this?" she asked, resolving to be more fun.

"Do what?" he asked uncertainly.

"Dance." She put on her most teasing, flirtatious smile. "I mean, are you sure you can keep up with me?"

Steve's pleased smile was as broad as her own. "Let's go find out," he said, pulling her toward the floor.

"This is nice," Guy murmured, his lips just inches off Nicole's hair as they swayed back and forth on the dance floor.

"Mmm," she replied, afraid that speaking might shatter the spell.

The first couple hours of the prom hadn't been the most relaxing experience, and now that things had finally settled down, she wanted to enjoy herself. She had already said hello to every member of Eight Prime except Jesse, who she'd been told had gone to some concert. Courtney and Kyle were off on their own somewhere, and Jeff and Hope were off on *their* own somewhere—hopefully in separate corners. All Nicole wanted now was to be left alone with Guy.

They were having a surprisingly romantic time. Guy looked handsome in his tuxedo, his black jacket emphasizing the russet tones in his hair, and he had admired her red dress with just the right amount of sincerity. Nicole felt completely transformed as they turned slow circles on the floor, the traumas of the past week gradually melting away. Melanie had been right: coming to the prom, acting like a winner, was the smartest thing she could have done. Her arms tightened around Guy, reluctant to let him go as the song drew to a close.

"Okay! We're going to speed things up now," the deejay announced, his voice breaking into Nicole's dreamy mood. Worse, the next song he put on was fast. Nicole forced her arms to her sides, only half-resigned to standing on her own feet again.

"Do you want to go out on the balcony?" Guy whispered in her ear. "It's getting kind of hot in here."

"Definitely," she said, motioning for him to lead the way.

She had noticed the lakeside deck through the lobby windows when they'd come in, but it had looked far too romantic to suggest going out there herself. If *Guy* wanted to go, though . . .

Just don't jump to any conclusions, she cautioned herself as he pushed open the exit door. *Remember what happened at the bowling alley.*

He probably just wanted to talk. Or maybe he really *was* hot. But once they'd stepped outside, and Nicole caught a glimpse of the starry night sky, she didn't care why they were there anymore.

"Have you ever seen anything more beautiful?" she gasped as they walked over to the railing.

All along the edge of the deck, glowing paper lanterns hung suspended from unseen cords, like stars that had fallen to Earth. Beyond them the real stars glittered, a swath of sequins across the full moon. And spread out at Nicole's feet, the glassy surface of the lake created a perfect dark mirror, joining the shapes of the real world above to the reflected ones below with only a shimmer of moonlight between them.

"It *is* beautiful," Guy said. "So are you."

Nicole stared at him, speechless. He had turned his back to the railing, to the lake, to all that incredible scenery. His eyes were only for her.

"I don't know if I should admit this, but I got

pretty jealous when I didn't hear from you," he said, reaching for her hand to pull her closer. "I thought someone else must be taking you to this thing."

"Well . . . uh. You could have called me," she reminded him.

"Maybe next time I will."

He pulled her closer still, his eyes intent on hers. His head leaned forward an inch, stopped, leaned a little closer.

He's going to kiss me! she realized. *Finally!*

Nicole's heart started racing so fast that she swayed on her high heels. Grabbing the rail with her free hand, she concentrated on holding herself absolutely motionless. Considering how long she had waited, this was undeniably big. This was huge, in fact, and she wanted everything to be perfect.

Guy's lips inched closer. She held her breath. They were just a split second apart.

"Nicole!" Courtney wailed from nearby, scaring them both to death.

Guy reeled backward and, if it hadn't been for the railing, Nicole might have taken a swim. Instead she spun around to see Courtney bearing down on her, watery makeup streaking both cheeks. Court's face was bright red. Her chest was heaving. Even a total stranger would have known something horrible had happened.

"Kyle *dumped* me!" Courtney cried, grabbing Nicole by one arm. "He just left with that heinous sleaze, Jillie Parks!" Furious, Court let loose a string of other adjectives for Jillie that made "sleaze" sound like a character reference.

Over Courtney's shoulder, Nicole could see Guy backing away. She winced to think what he was hearing, but he only motioned that he was going back in, to give them some privacy. She nodded gratefully, then turned her attention to Courtney.

"What do you mean, he left?" Nicole asked. "He couldn't leave without you."

"He did. He took Jillie and *left* me here."

Courtney's anger turned to despair. She collapsed into a sitting position on the damp wooden boards, fresh tears rolling down her cheeks. Nicole squatted beside her, doing her best to keep her dress dry, but Courtney seemed beyond caring about her own. She rocked back and forth on the decking, mashing green sequins beneath her.

"Maybe he's just in the bathroom or—"

"No! Nicole! I saw them go. He *told* me they were going."

Courtney dissolved into a fresh flood of tears, and for a minute all Nicole heard was sobs.

"It was her all along," Courtney got out at last. "It's *always* been her—that's what he told me. He was only with me to make Jillie jealous!"

"He . . . *What?*"

"I know!" Courtney sobbed indignantly. "I can't believe he would treat me like . . . like . . . He totally used me!"

Nicole put an arm around her friend's shoulders, uncertain what to say. She had never liked Kyle, or trusted him either, but she'd never expected anything remotely like this. Who could have? The only thing she knew for sure was not to point out the irony. Not with Courtney so upset.

"You're better off without him," Nicole ventured at last. "I know it hurts right now, but—"

"It *does* hurt," Courtney wailed. "And it's humiliating, too. Everyone saw us together, everyone knew about us . . ."

Nicole rubbed her friend's back, trying to calm her down. "I know. I'm sorry."

"Just don't leave me." Courtney twisted around abruptly to grab Nicole by both arms. "I can't go back in there alone. I don't even have a ride home!"

"But Courtney . . ."

What about Guy? What about the rest of the dance? What about the after-prom parties?

If there was anything worse than having a fifth wheel join her romantic date, it had to be a fifth wheel in such pathetic condition. Still, Courtney was her best friend. And no matter how many I-told-you-so's Nicole had saved up on the subject of Kyle, now didn't seem like the best time to deliver them.

"I won't leave you," she promised, smoothing a

red curl behind Courtney's ear and adjusting her green feather. "You just . . . you get this out of your system, then I'll go and find us some tissues."

"This is the last dance, so let's see all you couples out on the floor," the deejay said, cuing up his final song. "For you seniors, this is your last chance!"

"That's depressing," Leah murmured, barely lifting her head from Miguel's shoulder as they segued from one slow dance into another.

"What is?" Miguel asked.

"The last dance. Graduation. Everything's ending. People will be moving away. Life as we know it is practically over."

"Well, it's depressing when you put it like *that*," he said, shaking off the chill her words sent through him. "You're thinking about it all wrong."

"Really?" Her curious hazel eyes met his and he felt his heart turn over. "How should I be thinking about it?"

One arm tightened around her slim waist. His other hand guided her head back down to his shoulder. "*Don't* think about it," he said.

If she did, then he'd have to, and he didn't want to face all that. Not right now, at least.

All night, dancing with Leah, it had gradually been growing on him how deeply he loved her—and how lucky he was that she loved him back. From there it had been a short step to counting his other blessings. His mother was well now, and doing fine. His sister was healthy and happy. And with the salary Mrs. del Rios was earning and the money Miguel had saved, they would soon be able to leave public housing and be independent again. He had a lot to be grateful for. Somehow, in the shock of Zach's death, he'd forgotten how many things were still right with his life—and tonight he wanted to concentrate on those. He still missed Zach; he always would. But his girlfriend was a genius, his mom was doing great with her kidney transplant, and this had been the most romantic night of his life.

And it wasn't over yet. The prom might be down to its last few bars of music, but there were still friends to hang out with, parties to go to, pancakes to eat at the all-night diner by the highway, and a new day to watch dawn over the lake. Whatever else he and Leah decided to do, he'd make sure they were alone again by then.

He could just imagine her, standing out on their rock in her silver dress, mist rising in wisps off the lake all around her. She'd be like the heroine in an Arthurian legend, like the Lady of the Lake. He wished he could be her knight, sweep her up onto his horse, and gallop off to a castle where they'd live happily ever after. . . .

But, as she'd pointed out so often, things weren't going to happen that way.

And he wasn't going to think about them. Not tonight.

The last song came to an end. "Good night CCHS!" the deejay cried, waving from the stage.

The lights came up to sighs of disappointment, but it didn't take long for people to start clearing out, practically stampeding to the parking lot in their hurry to beat the crowd. Girls grabbed the star-shaped balloons off the tables as they went, giving Miguel an idea. Trotting to the nearest table, he snagged a silver balloon, then hurried back to tie its long purple ribbon around Leah's wrist.

"I would give you the moon and the stars," he joked as he did. "But I just have the one star tonight."

Leah's eyes twinkled. "We'll call it a down payment, then."

"Cute."

"Yes. You are."

Feeling his cheeks heat up, he quickly changed the subject. "So which party do you want to go to first? That one Melanie mentioned sounded kind of fun."

Leah shrugged. "It's definitely going to be the most popular. Maybe we ought to go there first. Then, when things start getting obnoxious, we can sneak off somewhere quieter."

"Quieter, huh? What did you have in mind?" he asked, putting his arms back around her. They were practically the only two people left on the dance floor now that the herd had reached the lobby. He swayed her back and forth, as if he still heard music playing.

"I don't know. Maybe a walk on the deck while all those cars are leaving? Who wants to be the first one to a party anyway?"

"Not me," he said, never more convinced of anything in his life. "Come on."

Taking her by the hand, he led the way through the back door and into the moonlight. The balcony had emptied, but the Chinese lanterns were still glowing, reflected in the water below like a string of colored pearls. Miguel walked out to the railing, pulling Leah along beside him.

"This was fun," he said, kicking a pebble off the edge and watching its ripples spread out in the lake. "I'm glad you made me come."

"I didn't *make* you," she said defensively.

"You know what I mean."

Her arms wrapped around him from behind. "I'm glad I made you too."

"We don't *have* to go to the parties," he said, wriggling around to face her. His arms closed a circle around her back, pulling her tight to his body. They were totally alone in the most romantic setting imaginable; he was in no hurry to move.

"What would we do instead? Stand here all night and make out?"

"Just an idea."

"Not one that's going to fly. We'd freeze our butts off out here. Besides, I *want* to go to the parties. At least for a little while."

"Oh." Even though he hadn't really been serious, he was still kind of disappointed.

"See, where you went wrong was with the all-night part," Leah told him with a mischievous grin. "If you had proposed, say, standing here and making out for the next half hour, then I'd have been your girl."

"You would have, huh?" he said with a laugh.

She brought her lips up to his. "Just try me."

Eight

"I'd like to take some time today," Reverend Thompson said, "to talk about an expression we've all heard at one time or another: What goes around, comes around. Most people probably believe this, but have you ever stopped to think about how Biblical that concept is?"

From her seat with the choir, Jenna listened intently. After her late night out with Peter, she'd yawned all through breakfast, but it had been the best kind of tired—the dreamy kind after a perfect evening. The prom had been everything she'd hoped for, and she and Peter had even found time to stop by a party before curfew. When she'd awakened earlier that morning and seen her pink dress hanging on her closet door, all she could manage was a sleepy smile at the memory of the fun they'd had.

Now, though, with one of her mother's thick waffles inside her and the choir all around, she was feeling more alert. It was great to be in church with her family—and Peter's—on such a beautiful morning.

Risking a peek down at the congregation, she saw Peter smiling back at her, and her heart swelled nearly to bursting.

"In the book of Matthew alone, there are several examples," the reverend continued. "Look at Matthew seven, verses one and two: 'Do not judge, or you too will be judged. For in the same way you judge others, you will be judged, and with the measure you use it will be measured to you.' In other words, what goes around, comes around."

The reverend flipped a page. "Or what about Matthew six-twelve? Our Lord himself taught us to pray to have our debts forgiven *as we have forgiven* our debtors. Look at six-fourteen: 'For if you forgive men when they sin against you, your heavenly Father will also forgive you. But if you do not forgive men their sins, your Father will not forgive your sins.' If we want to be forgiven, we must also forgive. What goes around, comes around."

He put the Bible down. "But my favorite example is Matthew twenty-five, and it's a text you've heard me preach before. Jesus tells us that the day will come when he will divide the people according to their deeds, and the righteous will be rewarded for their acts of love and kindness on Earth—for the poor they have fed, and the sick they have comforted. 'I tell you the truth,' Jesus says. 'Whatever you did for one of the least of these brothers of mine, you did for me.' When that day comes, our good deeds will come back to us in ways we can't even imagine."

The reverend paused, looking out over his congregation. "He also gives us a warning, though, saying to the other group: 'Whatever you did *not* do for the least of these, you did *not* do for me.' If we collect interest on our good deeds, then we collect it on our not-so-good ones too. What goes around truly comes around—good or bad—and magnified many times."

He paused again, to let his words sink in. Jenna felt the truth of every one as she leaned forward in her seat.

"So my message this morning is 'love one another.' Love your family, your friends, your classmates, your neighbors. Love the total stranger in need of your help. Love them fiercely, without reservation. Spread love wherever you can."

Reverend Thompson smiled as he came to his final point. "What goes around, comes around."

Mrs. Conrad stood up then to lead the next hymn, and Jenna raised her voice with all the force of renewed inspiration.

I think I do pretty well with what I send around, she thought, singing to her mother's direction. *And being in Eight Prime has been great that way. But I'm going to try even harder. A person can always do more.*

Outdoors, after she had put her choir robe away

and joined the rest of the crowd in the courtyard, Peter seemed to have been reading her mind.

"Listen to this!" he said excitedly. "Traci Evans is going to teach Eight Prime first aid and CPR! I just now asked her, and she said she'd do it for free. Not only that, but she has a friend who might be able to teach us water safety."

"Peter, that's fantastic! How did you know to ask her?" They were both acquainted with Traci from church, but Traci was at least ten years older than they were, and therefore not someone they hung out with.

"I didn't," he admitted with a grin. "Dad said I should try Matt Walters, and Matt told me to ask Traci. She's a school nurse and a Red Cross volunteer, so I'd call that just about perfect."

"I'd call it completely perfect if she's doing it for free. And we'll get our certificates and everything?"

"Yep." Peter glanced in the direction of the outdoor bench they usually sat on. "Do you want to . . . ?"

Jenna nodded and began to walk. "Well, that's wonderful news. I guess Traci was inspired by the sermon this morning too."

Peter smiled. "She might have been. I was."

"It's exactly like Reverend Thompson said. Traci's doing this favor for us, and we'll turn around and pass it on to the Junior Explorers, and who knows where they'll send it next? It's kind of fun to think about."

"Yeah. Plus Traci is one person helping eight people, and in turn we'll help maybe twenty kids—"

"And their parents," Jenna said.

"It's like a snowball effect."

Jenna thought a minute. "Maybe that's why things come back multiplied. The whole time they're out there, they're just getting bigger."

"Could be," Peter said, dropping onto the bench. "All I know is, I can't wait for our Eight Prime meeting on Thursday now. This is going to be great!"

"Am I believing my eyes? What in the world are you doing?"

The unexpected voice behind him almost made Jesse drop his paintbrush. Turning around at the top of the ladder, he looked down into Charlie's yard only to find Miguel looking up, an amused expression on his face.

"Hey, Miguel," Jesse said, his heart rate returning to normal. "What are you doing here?"

"I spotted you on my way home from mass. I thought you finished your chores with Charlie a long time ago."

"I did. But Charlie needed his house painted, and there's no one else to do it."

"You're painting this whole house yourself?" Miguel acted as if Jesse were crazy.

As if?

Jesse climbed down from the ladder and set his wet brush on a tray. "Mostly. Peter and Ben helped me prep yesterday, but they must be busy today. Probably all prom'ed out."

"Yeah, where were you? Peter said something about a concert?"

Jesse kicked at the grass. "It was just . . . a thing. Between you and me, I didn't really feel like going to the prom."

"Neither did I, at first. If Leah hadn't wanted to go so much . . ." Miguel shook his head. "I just have a lot of things on my mind. We did have fun. But this morning I woke up and . . . I don't know. I felt kind of guilty, I guess."

"I'm sorry about Zach," Jesse said, guessing what Miguel meant. "Stuff like that shouldn't happen."

Miguel picked up a dry paintbrush and flipped the bristles back and forth across his hand. "No, it shouldn't. The truth is, I didn't even want to go to mass this morning. I wouldn't have except . . . I made kind of a promise awhile back and . . ."

"Promises can be murder. I'm in the same boat. Parties all over town last night, alcohol everywhere . . ." Jesse pinched his thumb and forefinger together. "I came this close to going on the bender of all time." He shook his head, still barely able to believe he hadn't. "God knows I wanted to."

He wouldn't have been surprised by a lecture, but

instead Miguel offered a cynical smile. "I'm glad I'm not the only one hanging on to a promise I don't even know why I made anymore. It's weird, isn't it? I guess that's why they call it faith."

Was that what staying sober was? Faith? Jesse supposed that was one way of looking at it. Or maybe it was more like respecting the faith people had in him.

"I guess," he replied.

They stood looking at each other a moment, both suddenly uncomfortable with the seriousness of the conversation.

"So. You're painting a two-story house. By yourself. With a brush." Miguel smiled. "Do you *like* torture?"

"I must," Jesse said, thinking of Melanie.

"Well, don't let me spoil your fun, but I *could* make a phone call and borrow a sprayer. We could probably knock this whole place out this afternoon."

"Are you kidding me?" Jesse demanded. He had considered renting a paint sprayer, but they cost money and he didn't know how to use one.

"Unless you *want* to be here until Christmas."

"Oh, yeah. That's my one big wish. No, listen Miguel. Charlie's paying me a hundred dollars for this job, and I'm supposed to split it with Peter and Ben. But if you help me out, you can have my third."

"What? Then you'll be working for free."

"Free's cheap, believe me. I'd have paid to get out of this. You'll be doing me a huge favor."

"If you don't want the money, then give it to the

Junior Explorers. I didn't offer to help because I want to be paid; I offered as a friend."

"Fine. Good. But you're still getting the sprayer. Right? Friend?"

"Right," Miguel said with a grin.

"I have to mingle awhile," Mrs. Rosenthal said. "Will you be all right on your own?"

"Of course," Leah answered, waving her mom on her way. "Go do your professorly duty."

"I'll check back pretty soon. Or if I don't, your father will."

"I'm a big girl. I can figure out how to entertain myself."

"I know, sweetie."

Mrs. Rosenthal flashed her daughter a smile before walking off into the crowd that had gathered on the Clearwater University campus that Sunday evening. The faculty was throwing its annual barbecue for some of the school's top students, and since Leah's parents had to be there, they'd invited her to come along. At first she had declined, thinking she'd be too tired, but after spending most of the afternoon napping on the sofa, she had changed her mind. After all, hanging out with college kids would be good practice for next year. Now she surveyed the groups of students talking under wisps of low-hanging smoke from the grills, wondering where she wanted to start.

Those girls by the chips look friendly, she thought, feeling her stomach rumble. She and Miguel had eaten a trucker's breakfast of pancakes, bacon, eggs, and sausage, but that had been at four in the morning. She'd slept through lunch, and the yogurt she'd eaten when she'd woken up had just about worn off. *Or maybe those guys over by the fruit tower.*

She decided to start with the girls and began walking across the lawn to join them. Halfway there her father intercepted her, one of his students in tow.

"Hey, Leah," he called. "Here's someone you should meet."

Glancing back over his shoulder, he motioned a guy in blue jeans forward. "Leah, meet Shane Garrett. Shane, this is my daughter, Leah."

"Nice to meet you," Leah said.

"Same here," he replied with a grin. "Your dad's told me all about you."

Shane wasn't much taller than she, but the shoulders under his CU sweatshirt seemed easily twice as broad as her own. His hair was black and wavy, his eyes dark brown, and his smile impossibly brilliant. Deep dimples in his cheeks and one in his chin gave him a slightly impish appearance.

"Such as?" she asked, feeling suddenly nervous.

"Shane's transferring to Stanford in the fall, and I told him you're going there too," her father clarified. His expression reassured her that that was all Shane really knew.

112

"Oh, wow!" Leah said. "That's fantastic. What's your major?"

"Business. What's yours?"

"Philosophy. That's what I declared anyway."

"Philosophy is a walk on the slippery rocks," Shane said with mock seriousness. "I learned that in a song."

"Yes. Well, I'll leave you two to discuss those and other deep lyrics," Mr. Rosenthal said. "I'm supposed to bring the dean's wife a hamburger." He took off into the crowd, leaving Shane and Leah behind on their own.

"I wouldn't mind a hamburger either," said Leah. "I'm starving."

"I already had two," Shane admitted. "But that was just a warm-up. I can always eat more."

"Are they serving them to students already?"

"They are if you know the guys behind the grill," he said with a wink. "Come on, I'll introduce you."

She began following him over the springy grass.

"So, a philosophy major," Shane said as they walked. "I don't think I've ever met one before. What do you do when you graduate? Philosophize?"

Leah laughed. "Pretty much, I guess."

"You'll be a professor, like your old man," Shane predicted. "Personally, I'm going to knock them dead on Wall Street."

"You want to be rich?"

"Nah." He shook his head. "I want to be powerful.

I want to be *adored*. And if I happen to get rich in the process, well . . . I'll just have to deal somehow."

"I see," Leah said, smiling.

"My mom wouldn't mind, that's for sure. She'd have me set her up on the Riviera with a couple of twenty-something pool boys."

Leah felt her eyebrows go up.

"Don't look at me like that! My parents are divorced, so she's single. My dad's remarried—but I'll bet he *wishes* he were single. Oops! Did I just say that? Shame on me!"

Shane looked anything but reformed as he put both hands to his cheeks, Macaulay Culkin–style, his eyes twinkling with his joke.

"So tell me all about you," he said as they joined the buffet line. "Likes, dislikes, dreams, aspirations. Don't leave anything out."

"Well, let's see," Leah said, caught off guard. "I'd like it if you'd hand me one of those plates. I very much dislike coleslaw. I dream of somehow getting to the front of this line, and I aspire to end up with a meal devoid of raw cabbage."

"Ah, a short-term planner," Shane said knowingly. "You don't like to talk much, right? I'm driving you crazy."

"No. Not at all."

"That's okay. It happens. Some people are talkers, and then you have your reserved types. I'm not in that camp myself, but hey—I don't have anything against it."

Leah nearly laughed at the sheer irony. If Shane thought she was reserved, he ought to meet Miguel. He had already told her more about himself than Miguel did the whole first two weeks she knew him.

"I love to talk," she assured him. "I may just be a little out of practice." She was about to tell him why when a couple of girls in summer dresses sauntered by on the grass.

"Hi, Shaaaaane," they called, drawing out his name flirtatiously. One of them tossed her long hair in an obvious bid for attention.

"Hey, ladies," he called back. "Looking good!"

They giggled as they walked off, both clearly infatuated.

He is awfully cute, Leah thought, sneaking a sideways glance. *In a strictly academic, if-I-were-single kind of way*, she added quickly, remembering how romantic Miguel had been the night before. After an evening like that, she couldn't believe she was even looking.

I'm not looking, she told herself firmly. *I'm noticing. That's all.*

"So, Stanford!" Shane said as they inched toward the silverware. "I've wanted to go there ever since I was a kid and their marching band tackled a football team. How about you?"

"Um, maybe not quite that long." She wasn't even sure what he was talking about. "But for a long time. And I can't wait to live in California."

"Me either," he said with that impish grin. "Beaches and sunshine twenty-four/seven. I hope I can find time to go to class."

"You do know Stanford's in *northern* California, right? It's supposed to rain there a lot."

He dismissed her weather report with a flip of one brown wrist. "It never rains in California. I learned that in a song too."

Nine

"There's Kara Tibbs," Nicole told Courtney. "She made the squad."

The two friends had scored their favorite bench on the quad that Monday, but instead of eating lunch they were slumped listlessly against its back, watching the passing foot traffic.

"Her?" Courtney scrutinized the girl a moment, then lost interest. "Whatever," she said with a shrug.

"Yeah," Nicole agreed weakly. "Whatever."

She didn't know exactly why she was so depressed, but there was no denying the feeling. Maybe it was because the prom had only been a temporary distraction, and now it was over. Or perhaps it was because Courtney had been sticking around like a bad hangover ever since Kyle dumped her. Maybe it was because Nicole's romantic moment with Guy had been ruined when he had ended up taking her and Courtney home early. Or maybe it was just because a mousy-haired nobody like Kara Tibbs had made cheerleader and Nicole hadn't.

Which makes me even more of a nobody.

For a while, in the excitement of prom, Nicole had managed to fool herself into thinking things weren't so wrong in her life after all. Now, in the cold hard light of Monday, it all looked bad again.

"I don't even know what I saw in him," Courtney volunteered for the millionth time. "He's not even that cute when you take his personality into account."

"I agree," Nicole said, for the million and first.

"We are so over. I wouldn't take him back for anything. I don't even *like* him."

It didn't seem too probable that Courtney would have that chance, since news of Kyle's hot new romance with Jillie had already spread schoolwide, but Nicole nodded anyway, just as she'd been doing all weekend. Courtney was like a CD stuck in the changer—one that kept playing itself over and over and over. . . .

Nicole felt sorry for her friend, of course, but not as sorry as she would have if Kyle were worth all the drama—or if Courtney hadn't just been using him to make Jeff jealous in the first place. Then there was the whole issue of having warned her. Over and over and over . . .

"It's definitely time to move on," Nicole said numbly.

"Jillie deserves him," Courtney said. "The poisonous little tramp."

"You don't even know her."

"I know her rep."

So now Court cared about reputations. Too bad that hadn't happened before her own had become such a subject of speculation.

Nicole looked down at the lunch in her lap and thought about eating her carrot sticks, but chewing seemed like too much work. "Well, whatever. It's over now."

"It is *so* over."

They had lapsed back into silence, lost in their separate thoughts, when a shadow fell across their bench.

"Hello, Courtney," said Jeff Nguyen.

Jeff? Nicole's breath caught in her chest. Why was he talking to Courtney now, after what happened on Saturday? Was he out of his mind?

"Hello, Jeff," Courtney replied coolly.

Nicole found her friend's poise amazing, considering. If Nicole had noticed Jeff fawning over Hope at the prom, it couldn't have been lost on Courtney.

"So, uh, how are you doing?" His black bangs shadowed his eyes, but Nicole could tell by the way he was standing that he was nervous. He did have some sense, then.

"I'm fine," Courtney returned icily. "Why wouldn't I be?"

"You don't have to pretend. I heard what happened from Guy."

Nicole winced at his choice of the word

"pretend"—and did he have to implicate Guy? Jeff could have heard about Kyle and Courtney anywhere. If he'd torn his eyes off Hope for five minutes, he could have seen the whole thing himself.

"I'm not pretending. I couldn't care less." But the color rising in Courtney's cheeks told a different story, and her eyes had narrowed to slits.

"Yeah. Well. I just wanted to say I felt sorry for you, and I hope—"

"Sorry?" Courtney interrupted. "For me?"

Nicole squeezed her eyes shut and sank so low she nearly slid off the bench.

"You're the one who's sorry!" Courtney snapped. "Parading that pathetic wannabe around just because she looks like me. I don't know what kind of game you're playing, and I don't care. But here's a tip: The next time you want to make a girl jealous, don't hook up with her mirror image. Especially if her reflection can't dress and is having a perpetual bad-hair day."

"You—you think *Hope* can't dress?" Jeff stammered, offended to the core. "At least she's not trying to give the whole world a peek. And as far as picking someone to look like you goes, the only reason I noticed you in the first place was because *you* look like *Hope*! I've had a crush on her forever, and now that I have the real thing, why would I care about making you jealous?"

"You . . . you *pig*!" Courtney exclaimed. "You were just using me to get to her?"

Jeff shook his head vehemently. "At first I liked that you reminded me of her, but when you and I were together, I was completely with you. Believe me, it didn't take long for me to forget I'd ever thought you two had anything in common. You and I were over long before I got together with Hope."

"Yeah, because you dumped me to make it happen!" Courtney accused.

"You are so wrong. I broke up with you because I was sick of your attitude. I hate how cynical you are, and how pessimistic and—oh yeah, I forgot self-centered."

"I am *not* self-centered!"

"No? What do you call thinking my relationship with Hope is all about you? You know what, Courtney? I'm sorry I even came over here. I wanted to say something nice, but . . . now all I can think of is that you should get over yourself. Oh, and learn how to dress."

He turned and stalked off before Courtney could reply. Nicole watched as her friend half rose from the bench, then dropped back to the seat, her eyes filling with tears.

"He didn't mean it," Nicole said. "He just got mad and—"

"He wanted Hope all along," Courtney said, her

tears spilling over. "He was *never* trying to make me jealous. He didn't even care!"

"I . . . I'm sure he *cares* . . ." Nicole began lamely. But she didn't know what else to say. Unfortunately Jeff had done a pretty thorough job of speaking for himself. "I mean . . . well . . . *I* care," she fumbled, putting an arm around Courtney's shoulders.

"I am such a *loser*," Courtney sobbed, covering her face with her hands. "I don't even know why you hang out with me."

Nicole was stunned to see her friend crying so openly. Courtney had to be devastated to lose control in the middle of the quad. Even people who hadn't just seen her fighting with Jeff, who miraculously hadn't heard about the breakup with Kyle, were bound to see this and start more gossip. But to her surprise, Nicole discovered she didn't really care anymore.

She put her other arm around Courtney too, encircling her in a protective hug. "Because you're my best friend," she said.

Melanie hesitated in the gym Tuesday afternoon, watching Sandra enter her deposit check for next year's uniform onto some sort of fancy chart. The girls who had been in line before her had already paid and left. She and Sandra were alone.

"So. We, uh, have a pretty good squad this year," Melanie ventured.

"Sure do," Sandra said, still writing.

"Solid, I mean. Dedicated."

Sandra looked up from her ever-present clipboard to fix Melanie with a curious gaze. "I certainly hope so."

Melanie was nervous but took a deep breath, determined to probe a little deeper. "And even if someone did drop out, we still have a runner-up."

"Yes, but I don't expect to use her. I went out of my way to make sure I didn't pick quitters. The only way would be if someone broke a leg or . . ." Sandra trailed off, then shook her head. "No. Even then I'd have to keep the position open if there was a chance that girl could come back. It's only fair, after everyone worked so hard to get on."

"Right." But Melanie's mind was on a different girl, one who had worked just as hard, without the reward.

Sandra lowered her clipboard, clearly ready to move on. "Okay. I'll see you at the inaugural meeting this Friday. I can't wait to get our new squad off the ground!"

"Right," Melanie repeated dully, watching her coach walk off.

She still hadn't given up all hope of Nicole getting on the squad, but that conversation had certainly made her chances look slimmer. If only someone would leave town! But it seemed like no one ever left Clearwater Crossing. No one alive, anyway.

At least Nicole's acting more normal, Melanie thought, walking out into the sunshine and heading for the bus stop. *Or she was, anyway.*

Nicole had turned up at the prom in that knockout red dress she'd worn in L.A., and for a while she had seemed to be having a great time with Guy. But then that whole thing with Kyle and Courtney had happened, and Melanie had seen them all leave early. Over the last two days at school, Nicole had reverted back to her previous unhappy state—anyone who knew her could tell just by the baggy jeans.

I wish I could do something for her. If only—

"Hey, beautiful. Need a ride home?" The unexpected voice behind her startled Melanie out of her thoughts, even though she instantly recognized it as Steve's.

"Maybe," she said, slowing to let him catch up. "Hi, you."

"Hi, *you*," he returned with a dazzling smile. "Come on. My car's in this parking lot."

Melanie changed direction to follow him. "What are you doing here so late? Hanging around just to give me a ride?"

"Pretty much," he admitted, opening her door.

She got into the passenger seat and waited for him to walk around. It felt strange seeing him now, after the prom. Not that they hadn't had a good time.

If I wasn't insane, we'd have had a great time.

But the prom was over and, as far as Melanie was concerned, so were she and Steve. Based on the way he was acting, though, she wasn't sure he realized that.

I shouldn't have let him kiss me, she thought. *It obviously gave him the wrong idea.*

Except that how could a girl let a guy rent a tux, and a limo, and go to all the expense of a prom without even a kiss good-night?

"I sure had fun Saturday," Steve said, getting in on the driver's side.

Melanie smiled uncertainly, not sure what to say.

"You want to go out again this weekend? I know a great Mexican place. Do you like Mexican food?"

"Yes," she said, realizing too late that answering his last question had made it sound like she was agreeing to his whole plan.

"Good. And we can see a movie afterwards. There's a lot of new stuff playing."

Melanie hesitated, knowing she should set him straight. She liked him; she liked him enough to not want to see him get hurt. But there wasn't enough of a spark between them for a romance. The chemistry they had was more sparklers than skyrockets.

"Well . . . ," she said slowly.

He looked so happy it seemed mean to turn him down now. Besides, he'd taken her where she'd wanted to go. If they went to the movies, the score would be even. "All right."

"Great!" he said. "I'll pick you up Saturday about seven."

"Look at this!" Brittany exclaimed, bursting into Jesse's room with a back page from the local paper. The fact that he was trying to read on his bed didn't deter his stepsister a bit as she stuffed a photograph under his nose. "I told you the prom would be cool! I still don't get why you didn't go."

Of course you don't, he thought. Because he hadn't told her about Melanie, and he never, ever would.

"It was just a stupid dance, Bee," he said pushing the paper away, but not before he'd caught a glimpse of the Lakehouse Lodge lit up like a Christmas tree.

"It was not!" she insisted, trying to show him the picture again. "Look how romantic this is!"

"I don't know why you care. It's not like you missed *your* prom."

Brittany's brown eyes widened, and he knew he had hit the mark.

"You have to help convince Mom to send me to CCHS," she begged. "I'll die if I have to go to Sacred Heart for high school."

"Well, since you're only in seventh grade, I don't think we need to worry about your immediate demise."

"Very funny, Jesse. You know how she is. She

126

thinks public school is going to corrupt me or something."

"I know," Jesse said ironically. "She thinks it's full of people like me."

"Getting suspended didn't help."

"Well, hey. Tell her the fact that they kicked me out proves most people who go there are pretty straight. If everyone was getting kicked out, they'd have to think up something different, right?"

For a moment Brittany seemed to be considering his approach. Then she shook her head. "I'm not kidding, Jesse. You have to help me come up with something. Something *good*."

"But I don't have to do it tonight. I'm trying to read." Which was a lie, because even before Brittany had barged in he'd only been staring at the pages. Still, the last thing he wanted to think about was the stupid prom.

"Fine. I can take a hint," she said, pointing her nose into the air as she strutted out of his room.

Jesse tried to return to his book, but after Brittany left, concentration was even more impossible than before. He stared blankly a few minutes, his heart aching for Melanie, then tossed the volume aside in disgust.

You promised you weren't going to do this, he reminded himself angrily. *Why are you still thinking about her?*

In his mind, he started running through all the girls he could replace her with. One of the new cheerleaders was pretty cute: Debbie Something. Or that Robin from homeroom. Or Nicole.

Nicole would still pick me up in a hot second—Guy or no Guy.

He was sure of it. But a second later he ruled her out. Any fling with Nicole would be more about revenge on Melanie than anything else, and he couldn't use her that way. Again. Now that they were friends, it just wouldn't be right.

Besides, karma like that's bound to bite a guy in the butt sooner or later. If I haven't learned anything else about women, I hope I've at least learned that.

Getting restlessly up off the bed, he paced around his room.

No, what I need is a completely fresh, unjinxed start. Someone new. Someone I don't even know yet.

There had to be a girl like that out there somewhere, even in a hick town like Clearwater Crossing.

And he was going to find her.

Ten

"Miguel," Mrs. del Rios said, covering the telephone receiver with one hand and extending it to him. "It's for you. Dr. Wells."

Miguel's heart sank at the sound of his old mentor's name. His mother was looking at him expectantly, though, and he knew he had to take the call.

"All right," he said reluctantly, rising from the dinette chair where he'd been finishing some homework. "Could, um . . . could you give me a minute alone?"

"Of course, *mi vida*."

But her eyes were worried as she left the room, and he knew she was afraid of what would be said. His mother was sympathetic about Zach, but she didn't want Miguel to lose his job at the hospital. That he might quit on his own would be impossible for her to accept, so he waited for her to disappear before he lifted the phone to his ear. She'd find out soon enough.

"Hello?"

"Miguel? It's Dr. Wells. How are you?"

It seemed like a stupid question, under the circumstances. Did the man honestly expect him to be over Zach's death now? Because he wasn't. Not by a long shot.

"Okay. I guess," he said sullenly, resenting the fact that he was obviously going to have to repeat what he'd already told Howard. He wasn't going back to the hospital—nohow, no way. Why couldn't people just accept that and leave him alone?

"Glad to hear it," Dr. Wells said, a little too jovially. "We've all been kind of worried about you."

"You don't need to be."

"Maybe not. But the thing is, we all know how much it hurts to lose a patient. Believe me, you aren't the only one suffering over Zach. I still lie awake at night wondering what else I could have done, asking myself if there was some other way to save him. . . . If you think we're taking this lightly here, you need to think again."

Miguel's hand clenched down on the phone, but he couldn't think of anything to say.

"We just have to remember the bigger picture. We lost a battle, but we can't surrender the war. We all still have jobs to do." The doctor hesitated. "Which brings me to the subject of yours. I need to know your plans."

"I already told Howard. I'm not coming back."

"He told me you said that. I just thought now that you'd had a little more time to think about it . . ."

A little more time to get over it, he means, Miguel thought bitterly. Maybe the regular staff could shake off Zach's death, but he couldn't. Even if he could have, he wouldn't. Somebody had to remember.

"I was a fool to think I'd ever be a doctor," Miguel said angrily. "Or even that I *wanted* to be. I can't . . . it's just not . . ."

"You think I don't know what you're going through, but I do. Don't give up, Miguel. You've already helped more than you realize, and someday, when you're a surgeon, you'll be able to look back on your career and know you've saved hundreds of lives. But not every patient is going to make it, no matter what you do. Everyone dies eventually. It's hard, but it's a fact. Our job as doctors is to postpone the inevitable as long as possible, and to give our patients the very best lives they can have in the meantime."

The man's words made sense, but they also made Miguel shiver. Was that all people were doing on Earth? Marking time? Waiting for "the inevitable"?

"I understand what you're saying," he got out somehow. "And I know someone has to do your job. But not me. I'm just not . . . cut out for it."

"If I didn't think you were cut out for it, I wouldn't be talking to you now," Dr. Wells said. "But you have to make your own decision. If you're determined to give up the internship, you'll have to come to Personnel and fill out some paperwork for them."

"Okay," Miguel said, dreading the mere idea.

Wasn't there some way to do the paperwork through the mail?

The doctor cleared his throat. "On the other hand, those forms don't need to be done immediately. Why don't you take one more week? Take another week, and really think about it."

Like he'd been thinking of anything else! Still, Dr. Wells had just handed him seven days of stalling time before he'd have to go to the hospital, so of course he was going to take it.

"If you want."

"No, this is about what *you* want, Miguel. Or how about what Zach would want? Why don't you think about that?"

"Okay," Miguel said, just to shut the man up.

But after he got off the phone, the doctor's words stayed with him. What *would* Zach have wanted?

"What did he say?" Mrs. del Rios asked, walking back into the kitchen.

"Nothing. I . . . I'll tell you later."

Slipping out of the kitchen, he retreated to his bedroom and shut the door behind him.

Dr. Wells says he understands, but he doesn't. He can't.

If he did, he would know that not going back to the hospital was Miguel's way of honoring Zach's memory, of showing how much Zach's life had meant. Not only that, but the doctor himself had just admitted that sooner or later this would happen again—and Miguel couldn't be there for that.

Shuffling slowly across his bedroom, Miguel stopped in front of his dresser. There, in the bottom drawer, was the paper sack Howard had brought him, with the things from Mrs. Dewey.

He hesitated a moment, then carefully took out the bag and opened it. The green Wildcats hat Zach had worn to the end was on top. Miguel removed the cap with a trembling hand and set it on the floor, plopping down cross-legged beside it. The next item was a well-worn book. Miguel ran his fingertips over a snowy scene of a lone boy and his dog, then opened the front cover. Inside, on the first blank page, Zach had printed his name in wobbly, little kid's writing, followed by the words "My Favorite Book." Miguel's eyes filled with tears at the realization that Mrs. Dewey hadn't just gone out and bought him a book; instead she had given him something incredibly precious.

He finally took her card from its envelope and read the words she had written:

Dear Miguel,
I hope you will accept these things of Zach's with my lasting gratitude for the joy and comfort you brought him during a very difficult time. To the degree that his time in the hospital could be made brighter, you made it that

*way. He looked forward to seeing you every day, and I
know he would want me to thank you. Thank you for being there, thank you for caring, and thanks most of all
just for being his friend. He would have remembered you
always—and I believe that he still will.*

Very sincerely,
Amelia Dewey

Tears were dripping off Miguel's jaw by the time
he had finished reading. He hadn't thought he had
made any difference at all, yet here he was holding
the evidence: Mrs. Dewey thought he had. That she
could have written something so generous in the
time of her own deepest grief turned his silent tears
into sobs. *He* should have written to *her*. He should
have been the one offering consolation.

If he had been at the hospital when she'd come in,
he could have done just that. . . .

No. I'm never going back there. Even if his hours
hadn't been as wasted as he'd thought, he still couldn't
face that place again.

*After all, I'm only human. How much can one
guy take?*

"Nicole! Hi!" Guy sounded surprised that she had
called.

They hadn't talked since he'd dropped her off after the prom, four whole nights ago, so she couldn't
help thinking surprise wasn't a good sign.

134

"Hi," she said nervously, clutching the phone a little harder. "How are you?"

"I'm fine. How are *you*?"

She could tell by the way he said it that he was alluding to the problems with Courtney. Was he talking only about the prom, though, or had Jeff told him about that scene in the quad on Monday? It was Wednesday now, so Jeff had had plenty of time to go into every gruesome detail.

"I'm good," Nicole said quickly. "Everything's . . . better," she added, too embarrassed to ask how much he knew. The quicker all these fiascoes were forgotten, the happier she'd be.

"Well, I'm happy to hear that. You know part of me felt bad for Courtney, but mostly I couldn't help thinking it was only a matter of time. I don't know anything about that Kyle guy; it's just her attitude."

"I know," Nicole said reluctantly, not able to deny it. "Before all this happened, though, I really don't think she understood how people saw her. I'm pretty sure she's getting it now."

"I'll try to feel more sorry for her, then. Although she's still on my blacklist for interrupting us out on the deck. It would have been nice if Kyle could have postponed his big announcement five more minutes."

Nicole held her breath hopefully. Was he saying what she thought? And if so, why hadn't he called her?

"I miss you," she ventured. "I've been thinking about you all week."

"Really?" He sounded surprised again. "I've been thinking about you too. I just . . ."

Just what? she wondered anxiously.

"What are you doing this weekend?" he asked.

Nicole's heart skipped a beat. *Now we're getting somewhere,* she thought, anticipating an invitation.

"Nothing much. How about you?"

"Going camping with my family. We always go in spring, and then again in fall. Mom doesn't like camping in summer—she says there are too many bugs."

"So, you . . . you'll be gone all weekend?"

"Yeah."

"Oh," she said, disappointed.

"Why? Did you . . . want to do something?"

"No. Well. I just thought, maybe if you weren't busy . . ."

"Now I wish I weren't," he said. "I mean, I do have fun on these trips. But . . . I wish we could get together."

"Me too."

She wished it in more ways than one, she realized after they'd said good-bye.

Was it ever going to happen?

Leah hung up the kitchen phone. "What do you know about the stages of grief?" she asked her mother.

Mrs. Rosenthal was making a new recipe out of a magazine, but she put down the paprika when she heard Leah's question. "You mean that shock, denial, bargaining, anger thing?"

"Is that how it goes? Is that the right order?"

"I don't even know if those are the right stages. It ends with acceptance, I think. Doesn't it?"

"Not in this case," Leah said with a sigh. "Not yet, anyway."

"You're talking about Miguel."

"He just told me he's not going back to the hospital. He's been saying that all along, but now he's said it to Dr. Wells. I honestly thought he would change his mind. I thought he'd keep his job."

Mrs. Rosenthal picked up a towel and wiped her hands. "Why?"

"Because he belongs there!" Leah said, getting a little choked up. "He wanted to be a doctor so badly, and he'd be so good at it. I thought when he'd had some time . . ." She shook her head. "I don't know what to think anymore."

"Losing Zach had to be an awful shock. We never really know how we'll react to something until it happens, and then we just have to do the best we can. Miguel has to make his own decisions."

"That's just it! I don't think he's making a decision; I think he's in total denial. Somehow he's convinced himself that if he doesn't go back and face it, Zach isn't really dead."

"That doesn't seem very likely, Leah."

"I know, but it's true. Why else would he dump all his dreams?"

"They're *his* dreams," Mrs. Rosenthal said gently. "Just give him some time."

"I have," Leah said, still worried. She'd thought Miguel was snapping out of his grief at the prom, but now she suspected that had been the biggest denial of all. All he'd done was hide it, as if he had somehow stopped the clock for one night.

Now time was back on its regular schedule, and Miguel was quitting his job with Dr. Wells.

The next thing is, he'll be changing his mind about college, she thought, feeling sick at the mere idea. *No, that can't happen*.

She couldn't let him throw his future away. She loved him too much to stand by for that. Whatever the stages of grief were, she had to find a way to help him get through them.

But how?

Eleven

Nicole edged closer to Tanya Jeffries and Kara Tibbs in the lunch line, trying to hear what they were saying. Unfortunately, there were four or five people between her and them, making it impossible to catch anything more than snatches of the conversation.

". . . be there for . . . tomorrow?" Tanya asked.

Kara nodded. "Absolutely. I . . . fun!"

"It should . . . first time . . . ought to be interesting."

"Are you nervous?" Kara asked.

"I . . . big deal," Tanya replied with a shrug.

What are they talking about? Nicole wondered desperately. *Does it have anything to do with cheerleading?*

She thought about walking up and trying to join them, but she was afraid cutting the line would cause a ruckus. More than that, she was afraid Tanya and Kara wouldn't welcome her and she'd look stupid in front of the whole cafeteria. And then there was the little matter of Courtney standing right at her side.

"I think they're talking about that new cheer-leaders' meeting tomorrow," Courtney offered unexpectedly, without a trace of her usual sarcasm. "Tiffany was going on and on about it in chem today, saying how lame it would be. I got the impression she was just mad the seniors weren't invited."

"Oh," Nicole said, devastated by the news. After all, Tiffany was graduating; she wouldn't even be at school next year. But Nicole was the runner-up. If there was any slim chance of her ever getting onto the squad, shouldn't they have invited her?

No. Because there is no chance. Give it up. You're so pathetic.

The thought didn't exactly cheer her as she trailed Courtney through the lunch line, deaf now to the voices all around her.

Shouldn't someone at least have told me about it, though?

Nicole put a salad and some yogurt on her tray, more for appearances than anything else, paid the cashier, and followed Courtney into the main seating area.

"Where do you want to sit?" Courtney asked.

"I don't care. You choose."

Courtney found a table, and they were just about to sit down when Melanie wandered by. Alone.

"I just—I need to ask Melanie something," Nicole said quickly, dropping her tray to save her seat. "I'll be right back."

Courtney sighed. Nicole thought she heard her say, "Take your time," but there was so much other noise in the cafeteria that it was hard to be sure. One thing was certain, though: Courtney had turned into a kinder, gentler version of herself over the last few days. Being depressed had blunted her edge.

It's not doing wonders for me, either, Nicole thought as she hurried to catch Melanie.

"Hey!" Nicole got a hand on Melanie's shoulder just before she reached the condiment station. "Hi. What's up?"

"Not much," Melanie answered, a guarded look in her eyes. "What's up with you?"

Nicole glanced around, but there was so much commotion everywhere that no one else was listening. "I, um . . . heard there's a cheerleaders' meeting tomorrow. I was, uh, wondering if I should come."

"Did Sandra tell you to?"

"Well, no, but . . ."

Melanie shook her head. "I'm sorry, Nicole. But if you weren't invited you'd better not go. It's probably going to be boring anyway. Just a lot of gabbing about uniforms and camp and plans for next year."

Boring? Nicole would have *killed* to be in on a conversation like that. Once again the unfairness of the situation rose up to choke her with envy. "Oh. Uh, okay."

Melanie turned to go, but Nicole stopped her again, unable to drop it.

141

"It's just that if I *did* wind up on the squad, it seems like it would be smart for me to already know whatever it is you all discuss. Don't you think? Just in case?"

As usual, Melanie's face gave away nothing. Sometimes Nicole suspected she practiced that blank expression.

"Sure. But it's Sandra's call, so I guess she thinks it won't be that hard to catch you up. If she needs to," Melanie added a second later.

Was that a pause? Melanie had been the only one saying Nicole would still get on, and now she was saying 'if'?

"Have you, uh, heard anything, or has Sandra said anything, about anyone who might be dropping out?" Nicole asked desperately.

"Well . . . I don't know why I would have." Melanie glanced off across the cafeteria. "It's still early, Nicole. You have to be patient."

"Oh. Right."

"I have to go now," Melanie said, nodding toward the condiments. "I'm picking up catsup for my table, and they're waiting for me."

"Okay."

Nicole watched her walk away, even more depressed than before. Melanie was always cautious, but she wasn't usually evasive, the way she'd been just now.

142

It's like she knows something bad and doesn't want to tell me, Nicole thought gloomily. *I'll bet she knows I'm not going to get on. If I were, I would have been invited.*

On the other hand, if Melanie knew that for sure, why not just say so and put her out of her misery?

That's not possible, she realized, shuffling back to Courtney. *I'll be miserable either way.*

"Who's that?" Leah said, startled by a loud knock on the Rosenthals' front door. She scrambled up off her bed and hurried to answer it.

I hope it's Miguel.

Now that he wasn't working anymore, an afternoon visit was possible—in theory, at least. He'd never actually shown up unannounced before.

Leah opened the door with great expectations, only to be amazed. "Shane! What are you doing here?"

"How's it going?" he asked, flashing that dimpled grin. "Did you miss me?"

The truth was she hadn't thought of him once since the barbecue on Sunday. She probably would have eventually—especially when it came time to start packing for Stanford—but he wasn't exactly at the top of her mind.

"Oh, yes. I missed you desperately," she said, thinking teasing was better than the truth.

"Yeah? So how have you been? Keeping busy?"

"I guess. No busier than usual."

Shane shook his head. "I still can't believe you're in high school. You're so mature—and I'm not just saying that. You should hang out with some of the girls I go to school with. You could be their mother."

"Gee, thanks. That's every girl's dream compliment."

But Shane just laughed. "You know what I mean. You could pass as a graduate student, how's that?"

"Better," Leah allowed. "So what are you doing here?"

Shane held up an index finger, then frantically began rummaging in the book bag slung over one shoulder.

"*Voilà!*" he said, producing a typed report in a clear plastic cover. "I just stopped by to give this to your dad."

Leah stared. In her entire life, she couldn't remember any of her parents' students coming to the house to drop off homework. That's what faculty offices were for. How did Shane even know where they lived?

"Why didn't you just give it to him at school?" she asked.

"I missed class because I was trying to finish it up." He turned the report around so she could see his elaborate title page. "Fancy, huh?"

"You obviously don't know my dad too well if you think you'll impress him with fonts. He might even mark you down for putting style over content."

Shane grinned. "That wouldn't be very fair, now would it? I was born with style."

He tried to hand her the report, but Leah resisted.

"I really don't know if I should take that. You'd probably be a lot better off running it by his office."

"If he doesn't get this today, then it's late," Shane explained. "And I *know* he'll mark me down for that. I don't want to take a chance on shoving it under his office door."

"Well . . . ," she said uncertainly. "I guess it will be all right. But you'd better not make dropping work off here a habit. My dad can get pretty touchy about deadlines and following instructions and stuff—he's kind of old-fashioned that way."

"I can't believe I'm the first guy to ever bring an assignment by your house," Shane said.

"Actually? I think you are."

He looked surprised for a moment, but then he flashed that grin again. "Your dad's other students must not know about you."

"Excuse me?"

"If they did, there'd be a line down the hall right now."

"Very funny," she said, blushing as she held out a hand for his paper.

"So if I were to ask you out, would your dad mark me down for that too?"

Leah's jaw dropped. Was he serious? With Shane it was hard to tell.

"Definitely," she said. "You'd have to be crazy."

Shane laughed. "Too bad. Of course, the semester's almost over. . . ."

"Yeah, right. You say that to all your professors' daughters."

But her pulse kept pounding long after he'd said good-bye and she'd closed the door. It had been awhile since anyone had flirted with her so blatantly. Everyone at school knew she was with Miguel and left her alone. Shane was the first person she'd met who didn't seem to respect her relationship.

Probably because he doesn't know Miguel.

And then a new thought stopped her cold: Did Shane even know about Miguel?

She must have mentioned Miguel sometime during the barbecue. His name must have come up in conversation. She remembered she had started to say something once, but then some girls had walked by calling for Shane and . . . she was pretty sure the subject hadn't come up again. And if her dad hadn't mentioned Miguel, and she couldn't imagine why he would have . . .

"He doesn't know I have a boyfriend," she realized, laughing out loud. "Boy, will he ever be embarrassed."

Now that she'd solved the puzzle, she felt like she could enjoy the compliment without worry. Shane was cute, and older, and he clearly didn't have any problem getting girls. Not only that, but she liked talking to him. They'd probably be great friends at Stanford.

She smiled, and the motion made her recall Shane's dimples. Shane had a great smile, one that lit up his whole face.

Miguel has a good smile too, she thought loyally.

Then she sighed.

I just wish I saw it more often.

"Okay. So when does everyone want to do this?" Jenna asked, pen poised over her steno pad. "We need to make a schedule."

The Eight Prime meeting was under way at her house that Thursday night, and Peter had just finished telling everyone about Traci Evans volunteering to coach them in first aid and CPR. Instead of the enthusiastic response Jenna had expected, however, most of the members sat staring as if they hadn't even heard.

Melanie finally spoke up. "There's kind of a lot happening at school right now, so it's hard to know exactly what days I'll be busy. Stuff keeps coming up," she said, with a sideways glance at Nicole.

"Like what?" Jenna asked. "Now that the prom is over, I thought people would have time."

"Finals aren't that far away," Leah said. "And then there's graduation, and all the events that go with it."

"Yeah. I'm pretty busy," Miguel said, staring off over everyone's heads.

Jenna knew he was less busy than he had been for months, but she kept the thought to herself, sure he was still grieving Zach.

"How about you, Ben?" she asked instead.

"I can probably work my schedule around some-how," he said, as if that might take some doing.

Jesse snorted with laughter. "I'll bet."

"Well, I *was* really busy with the prom," Ben said pointedly, still milking his big date.

"Yeah, so are you and that Cheryl girl seeing each other now or what?" Nicole asked.

"I don't think so," Ben said grandly. "Neither one of us wants to be tied down."

"Yeah. Especially her," Jesse snickered.

"For your information—" Ben began hotly.

"All right," Peter broke in, giving Jesse an exasper-ated look. "Can we please get back to the subject?"

"How about you, Nicole?" Jenna asked, a little desperately. "What have you got going?"

"Absolutely nothing," Nicole said with a sigh. "I might as well waste my entire summer baby-sitting for free, because I don't have anything better to do."

"It's not a *waste*," Peter said defensively.

"And it's going to be a lot more fun than baby-sitting," Jenna put in.

"Whatever," Nicole muttered, not sounding a bit convinced.

"I think I'm free this weekend," Melanie volunteered. "Unless, uh, something comes up." She glanced at Nicole again.

"Look, we have to have some commitment here," said Peter. "I know people are busy, but free instructors don't come along every day."

Leah nodded. "You're right, and I don't mean to sound noncommittal. It's just that no one was expecting this, and at this point it might be better to wait until school lets out. We're not in that much of a rush, are we?"

"I am," Peter replied, his voice starting to get loud. "I've been telling the Junior Explorers' parents that camp starts the first week of vacation—which is what I thought we all agreed to. But we can't start camp if we don't have the certifications, and we can't get the certifications if we don't take the classes, and we can't take the classes if we don't have a schedule!"

"All right. Calm down," Jesse told him. "Geez."

"I can make it this weekend," Leah said guiltily. "We can, right?" she asked Miguel.

"I don't know. Jesse and I are finishing the back of that house on Saturday. Right?" he asked, looking at Jesse.

"Tuesday afternoon, then," Jenna said quickly,

naming one of two weekdays Traci had said she could make it. "How about Tuesday afternoon?"

She braced herself for the chorus of objections, but amazingly there were none.

"I can do it Tuesday," said Ben.

"Tuesday's good for me," Jesse ventured.

"Okay? Tuesday?" Jenna's pen hovered over her pad.

If there wasn't an enthusiastic chorus of agreement, at least nobody said no.

"We'll meet up at the camp after school," Peter said. "If anyone needs a ride, you can ride with me and Jenna."

"I will," Melanie said.

"I'll make some cookies," Jenna offered. "Does someone want to bring sodas?"

"I will," said Leah.

"Fine. Let's call that a plan," Peter said, with obvious relief.

It wasn't the most contentious meeting Eight Prime had ever had, but it had been right up there. Jenna was glad to close her steno pad.

What's wrong with everyone tonight? she wondered. Miguel being grumpy she could understand. And maybe Nicole wasn't totally over not making cheerleader. On second thought, Leah and Ben hadn't been that hard to get along with. But what was Jesse's problem?

Jenna sighed. *Sometimes I just don't get these people.*

Twelve

"Well, I think that's about it for the uniforms," Sandra said. "Any final comments?"

Melanie kept both hands in her lap, but it was a lot tougher to keep the smug smile off her face. She had carried the day on every single point of style and color. Next year's uniforms were going to be awesome.

"No?" Sandra asked, looking around the classroom where the ten new cheerleaders were meeting that Friday. "Good. I'll send our order in Monday."

She flipped a page on her clipboard, then pushed down on the metal clip to remove some colorful leaflets. "The next thing on our agenda is cheerleading camp. I have a couple different brochures here, and each camp has different programs to pick from. Pass these around, and look on with your neighbor because we don't have enough for everyone."

Sandra started the brochures both ways around the circle of chairs, giving a stack to Melanie on her one side and Tanya on her other. The two friends leaned forward to grin at each other as they took copies and passed the rest down.

"Cool!" Angela Maldonado exclaimed, catching a glimpse. "This is going to be so fun!"

All the girls started talking excitedly as the leaflets came around. Melanie opened her first one and smiled at a picture of three girls wearing shorts, the word SP-IR-IT appliquéd across their collective rears.

"It is," she said. "The whole year ought to be a lot more fun than this year was."

"Oh, definitely!" Lou Anne Simmons agreed, as if she hadn't kissed up to Vanessa every chance she got.

"Are we going to do stunts next year?" Becca Harvey asked Sandra, pointing to a brochure in her lap. "It would be so cool to take the stunt clinic."

Melanie tried not to notice all the eyes swiveling her way. She liked stunts as much as the next girl—maybe more. But Principal Kelly had forbidden the squad to do them after an extremely ill-conceived one had landed her in the hospital.

"We'll see," Sandra said. "We won't be doing basket tosses, but we may get off the ground again, once you're all properly trained."

The cheer that followed that announcement echoed in the otherwise empty classroom. Luckily school had already been dismissed for the day.

"I can do flips—front and back," Kara offered.

"Me too," several other voices chimed in.

"We'll definitely be exploring all our capabilities," Sandra promised. "We have a lot to learn about each other; that's part of what camp is for."

There was more excited conversation as the girls flipped through the brochures, looking at the pictures. There were shots of campers cheering and campers fooling around, as well as pictures of the dorms and cafeterias at the college campuses where the camps were held.

"Get me this room," Tanya joked, holding up a leaflet. "And make sure those are blackout blinds, because I like to sleep in."

"Thanks for telling me. I'll make sure there are *no* blinds on your windows now," Sandra returned with a grin. "We aren't going to camp to sleep."

"We're *supposed* to be learning cheers," Lou Anne said, as if Vanessa could still hear her somehow.

Rather than irritating her, however, the thought made Melanie smile. Vanessa *couldn't* hear them, and neither could Tiffany. Everyone on the new squad seemed pretty normal. Not only that, but with her and Tanya as cocaptains, no one would be able to turn into the dictator Vanessa had been, or even Tiffany's pain in the neck.

"Yes, we'll learn a lot of new cheers," said Sandra, "but the main point of camp is to get to know each other well, and to build the trust it takes to turn ten separate people into a single-minded team."

"Right," said Lou Anne. "I knew that."

"Okay," Sandra said. "I think that's all for to-day. Circulate the brochures around among your-selves, and next time we meet we'll talk about which camp, and when, and how we're going to pay for it. We'll only be there a few days, but be thinking in terms of keeping June free until we agree on the ex-act dates."

The meeting broke up with everyone smiling, ex-cited by the prospect of a great year ahead. Melanie shouldered her backpack, feeling more positive about cheerleading than she had in months.

"Hello, Co-Cap," Tanya said, falling in next to Melanie as they walked from the classroom into the deserted hall. "Is all this power going to your head yet?"

"All what power?" Melanie asked with a laugh. "Sandra's the one in charge."

"Yeah? I noticed who ran the uniform discussion."

Melanie grinned sheepishly. "You have to admit, they're going to be hot. Way better than this year's."

"Everything's going to be better than this year," Tanya said with conviction. "We're going to have so much fun. . . . I wish it was already September."

"Are you nuts? And miss summer vacation? Wish for June—that's good enough."

Tanya chuckled. "All right. But I'm still excited. Aren't you?"

"Yeah. I guess," Melanie said, wondering why Tanya had to pull the admission from her. She was cocaptain of a great new squad, they were going to have the best uniforms in Missouri, and Sandra—who was a reason to be glad all in herself—was taking them to cheerleading camp for the first time in CCHS history.

Shouldn't she be bubbling over like everyone else?

It's Nicole, she realized, as she and Tanya pushed out the exit door into a muggy, overcast day. *If Nicole had made the squad, I'd be ecstatic right now.*

As it was, she just felt guilty.

"I just think you ought to reconsider," Leah said stubbornly.

They were sitting in Miguel's car at Clearwater Crossing Park, too engrossed in conversation to get out and walk, as they had intended.

"I'm not going back there," Miguel returned through clenched teeth. "And *I* think if you cared about me, you'd drop it."

"But Miguel! You worked so hard—"

"Stop acting like my mother! This is my decision."

The way she pressed her full lips together told him he had hurt her feelings. Her hazel eyes filled with tears that caught the sunlight slanting through his dirty windshield.

"Leah, I'm sorry," he said quickly. "But you don't understand. If I went back to the hospital now, knowing what I know . . . It's going to happen again, Leah.

155

It'll happen lots of times. And you're not the one who'd be there."

She nodded, and the motion spilled a tear that ran down her cheek. Reaching over the gearshift, he put his arm around her and pulled her as close as he could.

"I was just trying to help," she said, her voice choked with emotion.

"I know." It felt awful to see her cry. "You have to stop this, or you'll make me start too."

She dragged a sleeve across her face and fixed him with still-wet eyes. "Would that be such a bad thing?"

Yes, he thought, worn out. He'd already cried all he wanted to. More than he wanted to.

"I just feel like there's a part of you that can't admit Zach's gone. Like you're still in denial. I know you'll probably always be sad, but you have to get on with your life, Miguel. Quitting the hospital is letting the cancer win twice."

"It's already won twice," he said bitterly, thinking of his father.

"But what about your mother?" Leah asked, reading his mind. "Doctors saved your mother's life."

She was right, he knew. So why couldn't he focus on that instead of the failures?

"Maybe if I could have gone to the funeral," he said. "Or if there had been a service or *something*. I never even got to say good-bye."

Leah wiped her eyes again. "If Mrs. Dewey had known how hard you were going to take this, I'll bet she would have invited you to the funeral."

He shrugged, thinking of the card she had written him.

"If you aren't going back to the hospital," Leah said, sniffing one last time, "at least promise me you aren't going back to work for Sabrina."

"I never worked for Sabrina. I worked for her father," he said, avoiding the real issue.

He had run into Sabrina the previous Sunday, when he'd borrowed the paint sprayer from her father. And since the back of Charlie's house hadn't been ready to paint that day and Miguel had had to return the equipment for Mr. Ambrosi's crews to use during the week, there was a good chance he'd run into Sabrina tomorrow, when he borrowed it again. He hadn't mentioned any of that to Leah, though, which only made her timing more uncanny.

"*With* her then," Leah said impatiently. "You know what I mean."

"I'd be a fool to promise that. Working for Mr. Ambrosi pays way better than any other job I could get. Besides, you said you like Sabrina now."

"What?" she protested. "When?"

"After the work party up at the lake. You said she was nice after all."

Leah made a face. "I think I said she was a good

157

worker. But whatever I said, I still don't want you hanging out with her every day. Especially not after I leave for Stanford."

"That's not for a long time," Miguel said quickly, flinching from the thought.

"Not that long. Not anymore."

"I won't even *know* who you're hanging out with," he accused. "You'll probably have guys hitting on you all the time."

Not probably. Definitely, he realized a split second later. The idea made him sick to his stomach.

"Like who?" she asked defensively.

"I don't know! That's what I just said."

She wriggled out of his grasp to sit upright. "I don't want to talk about this anymore. I thought we were going to walk."

She was out of the car before he could reply, taking long-legged strides toward the grass. For a moment he just watched her walk, trying to imagine he was some college guy seeing her for the first time.

I'd go for it, he thought. *Heck, I did go for it.*

Scrambling out of the car, he hurried to catch up. As miserable as he'd been the last couple of weeks, the only thing worse would be losing Leah.

How would he ever survive without her?

"That looks fine to me," Charlie called up from below. "Why don't you paint it now?"

"Do you see a sprayer?" Jesse asked irritably, climbing down from the ladder. "I'm just getting things ready for tomorrow, when Miguel borrows it again."

Charlie was hunched, red-faced, over his walker on the weedy grass, like a cardiac disaster waiting to happen.

"Hey! How did you get back here?" Jesse asked, suddenly realizing that in order to walk to the backyard, Charlie had somehow navigated the front porch steps on his own—something Jesse hadn't even known he could do. Then he had dragged himself all the way around the house on that walker, which explained why he was wheezing worse than a pack-a-day smoker. It was a miracle he hadn't fallen and broken a hip.

"I just wanted to see what you were doing," Charlie said casually.

"And?" There was no way he'd gone to all that effort just to see some stripped siding.

"And . . . maybe, if you're done, you wouldn't mind running by the store."

Jesse checked his watch and groaned. "Now? Everyone's just getting off work. The grocery store will be packed!"

Charlie's blue eyes flashed. "Forget it, then. I wouldn't want to put you out." He dropped his head and began laboriously turning his walker on the uneven ground.

"Will you let me help you with that?" Jesse snapped, annoyed by how guilty he suddenly felt. Grabbing the walker, he almost ripped it from the old man's hands in his haste to turn it around. "Cripes, Charlie. You shouldn't even be out here."

"Don't worry. I'm leaving," Charlie said icily. "Sorry to have bothered you."

"Oh, for Pete's sake," Jesse said. "It's not like I never do anything for you. I'm painting your whole house."

"I said forget it."

Later, on his way to the store, Jesse tried to focus on the fact that he and Miguel would finish painting the next day. After that, he didn't have to see Charlie ever again.

Or at least for a long time.

When he finally reached his destination, though, he still groaned at the sight of the packed parking lot. The lines at the checkout stands would be backed up down the aisles.

"This bites," he grumbled, cruising past without stopping. "I'm not going in there."

There was a mom-and-pop convenience store on the corner. Charlie would have a heart attack at the thought of paying convenience store prices—but Charlie didn't have to know.

Whatever the difference is will be worth it, Jesse thought, planning to pay it from his own pocket.

The bell on the glass door chimed as Jesse walked in, but there was no one behind the counter. He headed straight for the meager grocery section, intent on finding the stuff Charlie wanted before he forgot what it was.

"That's bread, peanut butter, Cheerios, milk . . . all right, now, where's the tomato soup? Don't *tell* me they don't have tomato soup," he muttered, juggling the other items. The milk was sweating and getting slick, and he was losing his grip on the peanut butter.

"Right here," a girl's voice said behind him. "Can I, uh, help you carry anything?"

"I've got it," Jesse insisted, even though his unsuccessful grab for the soup had nearly landed the milk on the floor. He fumbled everything back to his chest, not wanting to look incompetent in front of the teenage salesclerk.

Her name tag identified her as Mandi, and she was more than a little cute, with wide, gray-blue eyes and an auburn French braid down her back to her waist. A few stray strands curled around her face, making her look kind of innocent.

"At least let me carry the soup," she said, smiling as she turned and headed toward the register, the can still in her hand.

Jesse followed and dumped the rest of the groceries on the counter beside it.

"Can I help you find anything else?" Mandi asked.

"No. That's all."

"I know who you are," she said shyly, keeping her eyes on the register as she began ringing up his food. "You're Jesse Jones."

161

"And you're Mandi," he returned, nearly laughing out loud at how thrilled she looked before she realized he'd read her name tag.

She blushed scarlet, the rush of color overpowering the freckles on her nose. "I guess people must recognize you a lot. From football and everything. Bag?" she asked, flipping open a paper sack in an obvious attempt to change the subject.

"Yeah, sure."

Jesse studied her more carefully as she loaded up Charlie's groceries. She was maybe a year or two younger than he was, but definitely high school age. If she wasn't in private school, she had to be at CCHS. Still, he was pretty sure he had never seen her before.

He was pretty sure he would have remembered.

"You go to CCHS?" he asked carelessly, leaning against the counter.

She nodded, her cheeks still crimson, her eyes avoiding his.

"How come I've never seen you?"

She shrugged slightly. "I don't know."

"You're a big football fan?"

"Well, no. Not exactly."

"Then how do you know me?"

He wouldn't have thought it possible, but her blush actually deepened.

She likes me, he realized triumphantly, recognizing

162

the telltale signs of a crush. *She likes me, and she's got it bad!*

"I've just . . . you know. Seen you around school. I went to a couple of games, but I don't really get the rules."

"You just need someone to explain them to you," he said, trying out a flirtatious smile. "Someone who knows what he's doing."

She hesitated, then smiled back a little. "Really?"

"Sure. Football's not that complicated." He leaned a little closer over the counter. "Don't tell people I said that, though," he added with a wink. "I like to keep them thinking what I do is really hard."

"Right. I won't."

She folded the top of the bag over a few more times than necessary, then slid it toward him with both hands. "Here you go. Jesse."

"Thanks. Mandi."

"That's, uh, fourteen eighty-three."

He paid the bill, not even bothering to use Charlie's money. "Do you work here a lot?" he asked as he put his wallet back in his pocket.

"More than I'd like to. My parents own the place."

"Yeah? Because I help out this old guy I know, and he just loves to send me shopping. I might see you again sometime."

Mandi's smile stretched into dimples. "All right."

"If that's okay with you, I mean."

"I said all right," she repeated, giggling.

"All right, then." He smiled and stretched up to his full height, feeling more like a man than he had in ages. "I'll see you around."

"Bye," she said hopefully.

He strolled out to his car, tossing Charlie's groceries into the passenger seat as if nothing noteworthy had happened. But once the door closed behind him, Jesse chuckled contentedly with the thrill of his new conquest.

It had been so long since a girl had adored him, he had nearly forgotten what it felt like.

It feels good, he thought happily, putting the car into gear. *It feels incredibly good.*

Thirteen

This is a bad idea, Melanie thought, hesitating on the sidewalk in front of Charlie Johnson's house. The front of the wooden two-story had been freshly painted white, but the porch and the roof both sagged, and the landscaping looked more like mown-down weeds than anything planted on purpose. There was nobody in the front yard.

I should turn this bike around and pedal for all I'm worth.

She'd learned at the Eight Prime meeting that Jesse would be working somewhere that Saturday, and a couple of casual questions to Jenna had yielded the exact location. Now Melanie took a last deep breath, leaned her handlebars against the tree nearest Jesse's BMW, and set off for Charlie's backyard.

She found him squatting beside a pool of milky mud, cleaning paint from a brush with the hose. There were a few other tools lying around, but no sign of anyone else. Wet paint gleamed on the back of the house, suggesting the job had just been finished.

"So. You're done, huh?" she asked, not knowing what else to say.

Jesse jumped up and wheeled around, clearly startled out of his wits.

"Melanie! Geez! What are you doing here?"

The truth was she didn't really know. There was just this stubborn little part of her that still thought maybe, if she could talk to him alone . . .

Maybe what? What exactly do you think is going to happen?

"Why are you here?" Jesse repeated.

She shrugged. "I wasn't doing anything, so I thought I'd ride by on my bike. It looks nice," she said, nodding toward the paint job.

Jesse pulled a face. "That's because you're not looking closely. He's got rot in half those eaves, and we puttied over wood that's barely even there. You can only do so much when the guy won't spend any money."

"Well, he's spending money to get the house painted. Right?"

"Not really."

"He's not paying you?"

"A hundred dollars, for the whole job."

"Then why are you doing it?" she asked, surprised.

"Charlie's . . . not bad. Besides, somebody had to do it."

He likes him, Melanie realized, working to keep the smile off her face. *Deep down, he really likes him*.

"Well, it's nice of you to help out." Bracing her hands on the small of her back, she peered up at the eaves. The wood was in shadow now from the late-day sun, but she was still unable to spot any of the problems Jesse had mentioned. "I'll bet he appreciates it."

"Yeah." Jesse paused, his skeptical eyes meeting hers. "Why are you here again?"

Melanie tried to stay cool, but she could feel her face getting hot. She averted her eyes from his, skimming the rest of him instead. He was wearing jeans with ripped-out knees, and his tight black T-shirt was spattered with paint. His arms and cheeks were tan from his day in the sun, and his straight brown hair fell over his eyes in that way that made her heart melt.

"You know, if you had asked me to the prom earlier, I would have gone with you," she blurted out. "Steve just asked me first."

Jesse blinked, unable to hide his surprise. "What?"

"I tried to tell you before, but you didn't give me a chance."

He opened his mouth, then shut it, at an obvious loss for words.

"Oh," he said at last. "All right."

Melanie held her breath as their gazes connected

167

again. Then he abruptly bent back down and resumed cleaning his paintbrush.

All right? she thought. *What's that supposed to mean?*

On the other hand, what did she expect him to say? *All right* seemed as good as anything.

"All right, then," she repeated. "I guess I'm going now."

He nodded without glancing up.

She hesitated, wanting him to look at her again. For a moment there, for that one brief glimpse into his eyes, things had almost seemed normal between them.

"I'll, uh . . . see you around," she added.

He nodded again. "Later."

There was nothing to do but leave. Even so, she felt a huge weight lift from her heart as she retraced her path to her bike. If nothing else, it was a relief to have finally told him what happened. Maybe he wouldn't be so mad now. Maybe they could be civil to each other again.

Maybe we can even be friends, she thought, afraid to admit how much more she still wanted.

Swinging a leg over her bicycle, she started pedaling home. The sun was hanging low in the sky as she cruised down Charlie's street, and by the time she had coasted around the corner onto her private road, the fields behind her house were red with sunset. At first she didn't even notice the car in her driveway.

Then her eye caught a blond head hovering above its shiny black roof, and her heart nearly skipped a beat.

Oh, no. Steve! she groaned to herself, pedaling faster. *Am I that late, or is he that early?*

"Hi," she panted, rolling up behind his car. "Is it seven already? I guess I should have worn a watch."

Steve smiled, a little stiffly. "I was just leaving. Your dad said you weren't here. He acted like he'd never heard of me."

He was drunk, then. Melanie hoped she didn't look too panicked as she wondered how much Steve had seen.

"I am *so* sorry," she said, swinging off the bike and flashing him her most charming smile. "Just . . . would you mind waiting in your car while I run and get ready? I'd invite you in, but I'll just be in the shower. You might as well sit out here and listen to your stereo."

He didn't look too happy, but he opened his car door. "All right."

"I'll hurry," she promised, propping her bike against the garage and running for the front door.

Her father was nowhere to be seen as she sprinted through the entryway and up the curving marble staircase. She hoped he was passed out in the den, because she had enough things on her mind already without dealing with him.

I can't believe I have to go out with Steve right now, she thought, bursting through her bedroom doorway and heading straight for her white marble bathroom. *I should have just said no when he asked me.*

Why didn't I?

She wished she had, but it was too late now. Starting the water in the shower, she stripped off her bike shorts and tank top. A second later she was standing under the stream, knowing she had to hurry. Steve was out there, waiting for her. . . .

But in her mind she saw a brown head, not a blond one, and her heart ached with longing.

She was going out with the wrong guy.

Again.

"What happened to the Hershey's Kisses?" Courtney asked, sitting up in her sleeping bag.

Both dateless on a Saturday night, Nicole and Courtney had decided on a last-minute sleepover at the Brewsters', something they hadn't done since summer. Now it was more like Sunday, though, and after two videos and a constant stream of chatter, Nicole could barely keep her eyes open.

"I don't know," she answered sleepily. "You're the one who had them last. Maybe you ate them all."

"I didn't," Courtney insisted. "I ate all the licorice, I think. But not those."

"Look under my bed." Nicole rolled over to peer

off the side of her mattress, to where Courtney's sleeping bag was stretched out on the floor. All she could see was the back of a curly red head half hidden under the dust ruffle.

"Got 'em!" Court said triumphantly, reappearing with the open bag.

Nicole rolled back onto her pillows. "I'm surprised you're not already sick."

"Too much candy is the least of my problems," Courtney grumbled, stripping foil off chocolate.

"Well, I have a stomachache." Nicole rubbed her overfed gut through her nightgown, groaning at how enormous it felt.

"It was probably that extra glass of water you drank. Or maybe you just breathed too much."

"Very funny," Nicole retorted, bracing for more sarcastic comments about her dieting. But to her surprise they didn't come. Instead Courtney's face appeared over the edge of the bed, her chin burrowing down into the blankets.

"It's fun, hanging out like this," Court said, a little plaintively. "I'd kind of forgotten."

"Yeah. Well. We've both been busy."

"Don't remind me." Courtney's face slid back off the bed as if someone had pulled her plug. "I'm never going to fall in love again," she promised from the floor.

"You weren't really in love with Kyle. Were you?"

"I don't know. I guess not. But I thought we had more than . . . than . . . well. You know."

"Maybe Jillie will dump him."

Courtney chuckled, but she didn't seem as thrilled by the prospect as Nicole would have expected. "I'm not going to hold my breath. I don't even care if they stay together."

"You don't?"

"I'd still love to see him get what he deserves, but I have to admit I don't know what that is. I mean . . . maybe I brought this on myself. A little. What goes around comes around."

Nicole sat up in bed, stunned by her friend's admission. It wasn't like Courtney to accept any blame—no matter how well deserved.

"How do you figure?" she asked.

Courtney sighed. "I was using him to get to Jeff, and he was using me to get to Jillie. . . . Not that long ago, I was using Emily to get to you, although maybe you didn't notice."

"I noticed," Nicole said grimly.

"I was jealous of all the time you were spending with the God Squad. You know what, though? Since you started paying attention to me again, I've barely talked to Emily. I guess I'm lucky *she* didn't ambush me at the prom."

Nicole felt a wry smile on her lips. "There's always next year."

"Yeah, thanks."

Courtney rolled to face Nicole, propping herself on one elbow. "Seriously, though. I've been doing a lot of thinking, and this might be a wake-up call. It's like what they say—everything you do comes back to you sooner or later."

"What goes around, comes around," Nicole repeated.

"Exactly." Courtney sighed again. "From now on, that's going to be my motto."

"It's a good motto," said Nicole, pulling her blankets up higher.

Too bad Courtney had to suffer so much to come to such an epiphany, but if she had really learned her lesson, then maybe getting dumped at the prom wasn't such a bad thing after all. She had certainly been nicer to be around lately. Besides, there *was* always next year. . . .

"If I forget, you remind me," Courtney said earnestly.

"I will," Nicole murmured sleepily. "I definitely will."

"Leah! What are you doing here?" Miguel asked, opening the del Rioses' front door late Sunday afternoon.

Leah smiled mysteriously, but the truth was she was counting on the element of surprise. He would never go along with her plan if she gave him time to think about it.

"My dad let me borrow his car, and I thought we could drive up to the lake," she said. "The sunset was beautiful yesterday, and I'll bet it's the same tonight."

Miguel hesitated. "My mom and Rosa are over at a neighbor's. They ought to be home pretty soon, though, and they're probably expecting me around for dinner."

"Give them a call," Leah urged, walking past him into his small living room. "They might be glad to have a girls' night."

"I just . . . where did you say we're going?"

"The lake." She smiled invitingly. "You know you want to."

Interest finally sparked in his brown eyes. "I guess I could leave a note."

He walked into the kitchen, Leah on his heels, and scrawled a message on the chalkboard by the phone.

"Good boy. Now go grab a jacket and let's get out of here. Or you *could* show me your room," she added, suddenly curious.

Miguel had been in her bedroom, but she had never seen his. His mother was old-fashioned, and he had made it clear early on that bad things would happen if she ever found them together in there. But Mrs. del Rios was gone, and all Leah wanted was a peek.

"There's nothing to see," Miguel said quickly. "I'll just get my coat and be right back."

But Leah couldn't resist trailing him down the hallway far enough to catch a glimpse through his open door. Miguel was rummaging through his closet, which was on the same side of the room as the door, making him temporarily invisible. All she could see was the foot of a bed with a dark green cover and an old dresser with a wood-framed mirror above it. Then something on top of the dresser caught her eye: a Wildcats baseball cap.

"Is that Zach's cap?" she blurted out, forgetting she wasn't supposed to be there. Miguel had told her Mrs. Dewey had given the hat back to him, and Leah was sure that was it.

"Leah!" He appeared in the doorway, jacket in hand, and started pushing her back toward the living room.

"Let me see," she insisted, her plan taking on a new dimension as she struggled by him in the hall. Darting into his room, she picked up the cap.

"What are you doing?" he demanded from the doorway. She could tell he was getting mad.

"We need to take this with us." There was an empty paper bag in a trash can by the dresser. Stooping quickly, she picked it up, made sure it was clean, then carefully slipped the cap inside it. "Okay. Let's go."

She tried to leave, but Miguel stopped her at the door.

"Why do we need to take that?" he asked, grabbing her by her wrist.

Looking into his eyes, she almost chickened out. If she hadn't wanted to help so badly she would have. Instead, she took a deep breath. "Just wait and see, all right? You have to trust me."

The truth was she wasn't one hundred percent sure why they needed it, but she was already getting ideas. Twisting past him in the doorway, she hurried straight down the hall, through the living room, and back out onto the sidewalk. Then she rushed to her father's car and laid the paper bag in the backseat before Miguel could make her put the hat back.

"Come on," she called, spotting him in the front doorway. "Let's go."

The drive to the lake was quiet. Miguel didn't seem mad anymore, just lost in his own thoughts. And the longer he stayed silent, the more sure Leah became that she was doing the right thing.

I only hope it works.

Pulling into the main parking lot, she was surprised to discover that they weren't the only ones at the lake. Eight Prime had had the place to itself for so long that it seemed strange to have to share it, even on a Sunday in spring. On the other hand, the sun was almost to the horizon, and the only people she could see were picnicking far down the shore. Soon it would be dark, and they would disappear altogether.

"Come on," Leah said, pushing her car door open. She grabbed the hat bag from the backseat and tried to head for the water, but Miguel cut her off before she'd even made it to the grass.

"Tell me what we're doing here," he said, "because I'm starting to get the impression we didn't come to make out."

"No," Leah admitted, looking down at her sneakers. Then, steeling up her courage, she raised her eyes to his. "I've just been thinking about what you said, how you wished there'd been a memorial service for Zach, and then I thought . . . why can't we have our own? I mean, I know it's not exactly what you had in mind, but you wanted to say good-bye, and I don't see why the two of us can't do that."

Miguel didn't look thrilled by the idea. She half expected him to walk back to the car. But then he shrugged his shoulders. "How?"

"Come on," she said, taking his hand.

They crossed the grass, and then the sloping stretch of sand before the shore became muddy, turning to walk toward the big flat rock jutting into the water. Leah kept a lookout as they went, searching for the smooth, flat stones which were scattered about here and there. Soon she had dropped Miguel's hand to pick up the best ones, stuffing her jacket pockets.

"What are you doing?" he asked.

"You'll see."

He shook his head as if she were crazy, but a minute later she saw him sneak a couple into his jeans pocket, apparently afraid of being caught unequipped.

By the time they stepped onto the landward end of their favorite rock, Leah's pockets were stretching her jacket to her knees, and the sun was just about touching the water. She walked out to the rock's end, the bag with Zach's hat still clutched in one hand and her other hand back in Miguel's. They stood with the water lapping inches from their feet, watching the setting sun turn the ripples pink and orange.

"You were right; it's a good sunset," Miguel said at last. "But I'm not sure what that has to do with Zach."

Dropping his hand, she reached into her pocket and took out a water-smooth stone.

"I do remember Zach," she said. "I remember the way he made you smile." With a quick, strong flick of her wrist, she sent the stone skipping far out over the lake, setting off concentric bursts of ripples everywhere it touched.

Miguel was staring at her, a strange expression on his face. She took out another stone.

"I remember sitting in the ICU waiting room with his mother that time his heart stopped, and how scared we all were, and how obviously she loved him." Leah sidearmed her second stone, getting even more skips than she had from the first one.

Miguel was still staring.

"You do one," she urged. She tried to hand him a stone, but he shook his head.

Then, slowly, he pulled one from his own pocket.

"I remember how brave he was. He was the bravest kid in the world." The power Miguel put behind his stone sent it an amazing distance between bounces. Leah finally lost sight of it against the setting sun.

"Do it again," she whispered.

Miguel took out his second stone. "I remember how he never complained, even when he should have."

That stone disappeared as well and Leah handed him another.

"I remember the way he used to light up when I stopped by." He fired off the third stone, the beginnings of tears on his cheeks as he reached for another.

"And teaching him chess . . . and the way his baby teeth showed when he laughed . . . and how I thought I could be his big brother . . ." A stone went off behind every memory, as Miguel's tears streamed more freely. Leah was crying too as she handed them over one by one.

"I remember finding out he was back in ICU . . . and Howard's face when he told me . . . and all the plans we had that are never going to happen!"

Miguel threw the last stone overhand, aiming angrily straight at the sun. Then, turning to Leah, he gathered her into his arms and wept. She squeezed him back with her own tears wetting her face, half sorrow and half relief. She had seen anger just now, and she had seen heartbreak . . . but she hadn't seen denial.

When at last Miguel's tears died down, she stepped back and took Zach's cap from the bag. The sun had gone completely below the horizon, but there was still enough light to see by as she held the hat out between them. When she'd picked it up at his house, she'd been thinking vaguely in terms of floating it out onto the darkened lake, like a Viking funeral ship. Now she had a better idea. Releasing the back strap from Zach's small size, she reached up and put the cap on Miguel's head.

He looked at her questioningly.

"I have a ring from my grandmother," she said. "She left it to me so that I can remember her anytime I wear it. Zach left you his hat, and I think you ought to wear it the same way."

"Yeah?" he asked, looking uncertain.

"Definitely," she said, snuggling back into his arms.

She felt him relax up against her, breathing deep down into his lungs. And even though he didn't say anything else, she allowed herself to hope.

She knew Miguel was still grieving. He probably would be a long time.

But she thought he had finally found some peace.

Fourteen

"Melanie! Hey, Melanie, wait up!"

Melanie cringed, recognizing the voice behind her as Steve's. She had managed to avoid him all Monday, but now that school was out he had finally caught up with her halfway across CCHS's front lawn.

Great. Perfect.

The problem wasn't Steve so much as the way he was clinging to her lately. They'd gone to dinner and the movies on Saturday, and that had been all right, but once he'd brought her home it had taken an hour to get rid of him. All she had wanted was to be alone, to go up to bed and dream of Jesse. But even after she'd kissed him good night, Steve had kept hanging around her front door, angling to come in.

As if there was any way with Dad drinking. She sighed as Steve ran the last few feet to where she stood, eagerness all over his face. *As if there was any way anyway.*

"Hey, why are you walking way over here?" he asked. "You can't be taking the bus?"

"I usually do," she answered, looking longingly toward the stop on the corner.

"Don't even think about it! I'll drive you."

Grabbing one of her hands, he tried to pull her toward the student parking lot, but she dug in her heels.

"What's the matter?" he asked when she didn't move. "I'm just parked right over there."

"I can't go out with you anymore," she blurted. "It's over."

"What?" He couldn't have looked more stunned if she had slapped him across the face. "I don't understand. What did I do?"

"You didn't do anything. It's just . . . I wanted to go to the prom with you—and I had a great time. But I was never really thinking in terms of more than that. You're trying to turn this into some whole big relationship, and it just doesn't exist."

Steve let go of her hand. "But I thought . . . This is . . . I *like* you, Melanie. I thought that you liked me."

She felt like running for cover, but instead she hiked her backpack higher on her shoulders, determined to hold her ground. If she didn't want to have this conversation again, she needed to finish it now.

"I do like you. As a friend."

Steve's head rolled back. His eyes closed with the pain of rejection.

"You're a nice guy," she added quickly. "But you

really don't know me that well. There are a lot of things going on in my life. Believe me, you don't want to get involved."

"How do you know?" he flung back, wounded. "Maybe I thought I was already involved!"

Melanie glanced around nervously, hoping no one was listening. Students were walking in two's and three's across the lawn, but most were headed to the parking lot. None seemed to be watching her and Steve.

"It's just . . . it's better this way," she told him, a trace of desperation in her voice.

"Better how?" he demanded. "Better for who?" He looked down at the grass, and when he raised his head again there were tears in his blue eyes.

"Steve, you're taking this too hard!" After all, they had only gone out a couple of times . . . and what if somebody saw him crying? Did he have no pride at all?

"It *is* hard," he said, roughly wiping his eyes. They spilled over anyway, making tracks down his cheeks.

Reaching forward impulsively, she took both his hands in hers. "I'm really sorry, Steve. I never meant to hurt you."

"No?" he said hopefully. With a yank, he pulled her to his chest and wrapped his arms around her. "Then don't," he begged into her hair. "Don't do this, Melanie."

This is a nightmare, she thought, stiffening in his embrace. Her previous concern about people seeing him cry seemed like small potatoes in the face of such a blatant, one-sided public display of affection. She had heard many times that it was better to break up with people in crowded places, so they couldn't make a scene, but Steve either had never heard that rule or didn't care.

"I just . . . I think I *love* you," he whimpered.

"You don't mean that."

"No, I do," he insisted, more loudly. "Just give me a chance, Melanie."

His arms tightened around her as if he'd have to be pried off. At that moment she would have paid any price to be somewhere far, far away. But the longer he held on, the sorrier she was for the unintended pain she'd caused . . . and the more touched by the depth of his feelings.

"Don't be sad," she begged, tentatively returning his hug. "Really. It's not worth it."

Steve didn't say anything.

"We'll go back to being friends, and everything will be fine," she insisted, hearing the strain in her voice.

"Just give me another chance," he said stubbornly. "A *real* chance, Melanie."

She closed her eyes, out of ideas. She had dated lots of guys once or twice, then moved on. Sometimes they were the ones who moved on. It had never been a big deal before. After all, two dates didn't constitute a relationship. That was the *point* of dating, wasn't it? A date was like a test drive—not everyone bought the car.

So why was she suddenly wondering if she was doing the right thing? Was it possible she was being too hasty?

This is almost exactly what happened with Jesse. And I'm still regretting that.

Her arms tightened around Steve.

Maybe I should give him a better chance.

"There it is!" Jesse exclaimed, relieved to have spotted Miguel's hammer lying against the back foundation of Charlie's house. "I can't believe I didn't see that when I picked up the tools Saturday."

"No problem," Miguel said calmly, bending to retrieve it. "I didn't see it either."

"Is it all right?" Jesse asked. "Not rusted or anything?"

Miguel wiped the tool on his jeans. "It's fine."

"Good. Then let's go tell Charlie we found it, and we can get out of here."

Back in the front yard, Charlie was waiting on the porch, hunched over his walker. "Did you find it?" he asked as the guys rounded the corner.

"Yeah. It was back there," Jesse said.

"I told you I didn't have it!" Charlie said triumphantly.

"Well, I didn't think you had taken it. I only asked if you'd seen it."

In retrospect, Jesse couldn't help thinking it would have been a lot easier to sneak into the backyard and look for the hammer without knocking. Unfortunately, he *had* knocked, and now Charlie was sure to give him and Miguel the third degree before they got out of there.

"This guy's pretty lucky you came along with that sprayer," Charlie told Miguel, tilting his head toward Jesse. "He'll think twice before he takes on another big job like this without the proper equipment. You can't make any money that way."

Miguel smiled, amused, while Jesse ground his teeth.

"Okay. We're leaving now," Jesse announced.

"You know, you boys did a real nice job," Charlie said, maneuvering his walker to the edge of the porch so he could admire the front of the house. "I ought to sell this old place now, while it looks so good."

"What?" Jesse said, surprised.

"Why do you want to sell it?" asked Miguel.

Charlie shrugged his bony shoulders. "I'm going to have to sell it pretty soon anyway. It's been years since I've been able to use the upstairs, and it's harder and harder for me to get around downstairs now, too. It doesn't make any sense for me to rattle around this big place when I can't even get my own groceries."

Was that a hint? Jesse wondered. *Is he just trying to get me to take him shopping?*

Shopping with Charlie wasn't the most enticing prospect, but shopping *for* him wasn't a huge big deal. Especially not when Mandi's parents owned a convenience store. Jesse had still only seen her that once . . . but there was no time like the present.

"I could help with groceries more often," he said, managing not to sound too eager. "In fact, I could go now, if you want."

Charlie smiled. "Thanks, but it's getting more complicated than that. No, what I need is a nice nursing home, with lots of pretty nurses, and maids, and a real cook."

He looked up at his house again, then nodded thoughtfully. "If I sold this place, I could afford it, too. Problem is, the neighborhood isn't what it used to be. It's going to take a lot of young blood moving in here, fixing things up, to put this street back in shape. I'd probably have to carry paper even to make the sale."

Charlie paused a moment, mulling it over. "I could do that, though. For the right person. It might even be to my advantage."

"That's good," Jesse said, not sure how else to answer. The old guy was rambling—and he probably wasn't even serious. "We'll see you around, Charlie. Maybe I'll stop by next week."

"Okay," Charlie said, waving distractedly. He thumped and scraped his walker laboriously to his door, then disappeared inside.

"What was he talking about?" Miguel asked as he and Jesse walked out to the curb. "Is he really going to sell that place?"

"Who knows. Charlie is . . . Charlie."

"But what was all that other stuff he was saying? What does 'carry paper' mean?"

"I have no idea. Whatever it means is sure to be boring."

"We should ask him," Miguel said.

"Why do you care?"

"I don't. Just curious."

"Then look it up in the dictionary or something, because no way am I getting that guy yakking again. Come on, let's get out of here."

"Home at last!" Leah sighed, walking into the lobby of the Rosenthals' condominium building. "Another Monday bites the dust."

She and Miguel had eaten lunch together at school that day, and even if he hadn't seemed completely back to normal, the change was enough of a relief that she had been able to research a term paper in the library all afternoon without worrying about him. Now the sky was getting dark, though, and Leah was in a hurry to get upstairs and start dinner before her parents came home from work. She headed for the staircase, then abruptly changed direction and stopped at her family's mailbox instead.

"Might as well grab this stuff," she muttered, wondering if there would be anything for her. There usually wasn't, but that day as she unlocked the box, she just had a premonition. . . .

"Aha!" she said, discovering an envelope with her name on it amid the other mail. She didn't recognize the handwriting, and she tore it open eagerly, curious to see who it was from. Inside was a piece of lined notebook paper. She pulled it out, and a red window decal slipped from between the folds, fluttering to her feet.

"Stanford," she said softly, recognizing the logo as she bent to pick it up. "I know who this is from."

Her eyes went straight to the bottom of the page and, sure enough, the signature was Shane's. She scanned back up to the top to read what he had written:

Hey, Leah!
Just a little something to psych you up.
Rah rah, and all that.
Personally, I can't wait!
Shane

Leah shook her head, smiling at the decal in her hand. Shane was a total goof, but she had to admit his enthusiasm was infectious.

He had a lot of things going for him, actually. He was cute, smart enough to get into Stanford, and one of the most confident people she'd ever met. He was incredibly open and easy to talk to. But most of all, he had the type of true ambition she'd have given anything to see in Miguel.

He's my dream guy, basically. If I wasn't with Miguel . . .

The thought startled her out of her reverie. Gathering up the mail, she shut the mailbox door and hurried toward the staircase.

I am with Miguel, she reminded herself, taking the stairs two at a time. *I love Miguel.*

She couldn't believe she'd had such a disloyal thought.

It meant nothing, she reassured herself, slamming out of the stairwell on the fourth floor. *It only happened because I was thinking of college. Because Shane's going to be there. And Miguel isn't.*

So why was her heart racing as she fumbled with her front door? Why did she feel as guilty as if she and Shane had been caught in some illicit act? Why did she run straight to her room and bury his note at the deep, dark bottom of a drawer?

Because it didn't feel like nothing.

Fifteen

"This is going to be so fun!" Jenna said, snapping the folding card table upright and setting it against one wall of the little cabin at the lake. In school that Tuesday, all she'd been able to think about was the Eight Prime meeting that afternoon, and now it was finally about to start. Everyone was there, although most of the group was outside, and as soon as Traci showed up, their first class would get under way.

Leah started putting sodas onto the table. "Have you ever taken first aid?" she asked skeptically. "It's not fun if you're squeamish."

"I'm not," Jenna said.

"I am," said Nicole. "This isn't going to be gross, is it?"

Peter walked inside just long enough to grab one of the cookies Jenna was piling onto a plate. "Nothing's gross if it saves a life."

"Says you," Nicole muttered as he left again. "I heard that when you're doing rescue breathing, the other person can throw up right into your mouth.

192

I don't care what Peter says—that's gross by any standard."

"Eew," Jenna said, feeling her throat close up. "That *is* pretty gross."

Melanie wandered in then and came over to the table. "What are you talking about?"

"Believe me, you don't want to know," Leah told her.

"Well, Traci just got here, and Peter wants everyone out at the flagpole," Melanie said. "The guys are already out there."

"What?" Jenna protested. "I just got the snacks set up in here."

Melanie shrugged. "They want to use the benches, since the weather's nice and there's more room. We can always break for cookies later."

"Someone could have told me," Jenna grumbled.

But by the time the girls had walked out into the sunshine, crossing the packed-dirt clearing to the split-log benches under the flagpole, Jenna had forgotten all about cookies in the excitement of getting started on her counselor certifications.

Traci was standing with one sandal up on the first bench, a stack of paperback booklets in her hand. The guys had taken seats in front of her and were already looking at copies.

"Hey, Traci!" Jenna greeted her cheerfully. "You made it!"

"Was there some doubt about that?" their instructor asked, smiling, as she passed out booklets to the girls. She was wearing pink shorts and a sleeveless shirt, making Jenna think she must have changed clothes after work. Her short dark hair was pulled into a two-inch ponytail.

"I'm just excited to see you," Jenna said. "Did you already meet Melanie? This is Leah, and Nicole."

Everyone said hello, and then the girls took seats behind the guys and the whole group looked expectantly at Traci.

"We're going to talk about first aid this afternoon," she announced. "It's a lot of material, but if we keep on track and don't digress too much, we ought to be able to cover it all today. The CPR certification takes about six hours, so we'll do that over two more afternoons, or maybe on a weekend. You'll do water safety last, with another instructor. Any questions?"

Ben's hand shot into the air. "Do we need red bathing suits for that?"

"What?" Traci looked mystified. "Why would they have to be red?"

Jenna suppressed a smile. *Welcome to Ben 101*, she thought.

"Lifeguards always wear red," Ben said. "And since we'll be in lifeguard training . . ."

"Any suit that stays on will be fine. Plus Lifeguard is a step or two above the certification you'll be getting." Traci turned to Peter. "I thought you said your older brother was taking Red Cross Head Lifeguard training."

"He is," Peter confirmed. "He signed up for the classes already, and he'll have it all done before he gets home for the summer."

Traci nodded. "The class you'll all be taking is more of an assistant lifeguard thing made up by the parks department, but you'll learn more about that later. You'll still want David around anytime the kids go swimming."

"Once, when I was little, the lifeguard at the plunge had to jump in and save me," Ben reported.

"Why doesn't that surprise me?" Jesse asked. "Anyway, I thought we were supposed to be doing first aid now."

"Yes. Can we get on with that?" Nicole asked impatiently.

"If everybody's ready." Traci paused a moment, her eyes on someone, and Jenna followed her gaze. Miguel was gazing off into space, lost in his own private world.

Even more private than usual, Jenna thought, realizing she hadn't heard him say a single word yet that afternoon. *What's on his mind?* she wondered.

Zach seemed the most likely possibility, although Miguel didn't look quite so sad anymore. It was more like he was mulling something over. . . .

"Miguel, are you with us?" Traci asked.

He jumped, clearly startled. "Yeah. Go ahead."

"All right." Traci opened her book and told everyone what page to turn to. "If you look at this little chart here, you see there are three important steps to follow in any first aid emergency. The steps are Check, Call, and Care. See? They're easy to remember, because they all start with a C."

She lowered her book and kept talking. "So what's the first thing we do in an emergency injury situation? We check the scene and the victim. We try to find out if there is any more danger present, and the exact nature of the person's injuries. We want to check carefully, but we need to check quickly because the next step is to call 911. You want to make that call as fast as you can, and in an extreme emergency, where injuries are sure to be severe, you may even call *before* you check."

"If two people were helping, one could go make the call while the other checked," Jenna said.

"Yes. Although it's definitely helpful if you can tell the 911 operator exactly what the problem is. Sometimes, if the phone is near the victim, the operator can stay on the line and tell you what to do until a medic arrives. Which brings us to the third step: care. Once the call has been made, you need to care for the victim until help arrives, usually in the form of an ambulance."

"Oh!" Ben said, his arm in the air again. "When I was ten, I fell off my bike, and our neighbor saw from a window and called 911."

"Were you hurt?" Traci asked.

"Not really," Ben admitted.

"Now *there's* a fascinating story," Jesse said under his breath.

"Well, it's better to be safe," Traci said. "Still, if your neighbor had checked first, she might have realized that she didn't need to call 911."

"It says on the next page when you're supposed to call for an ambulance," Leah said, skipping ahead.

"Right. There are certain situations where you should always call, no matter what."

Traci lifted her book again and began reading down a list that made Jenna shiver—things like broken bones, seizures, and severe bleeding. Jenna really, really hoped they'd never have one of those situations at camp.

"Another place you don't want to take a chance is with head injuries," Traci continued. "Head and neck injuries are always potentially serious, especially if the person becomes unconscious."

Tell me about it, Jenna thought, remembering the terror of Sarah's coma after she had been hit by a drunk driver. Peter glanced over his shoulder at her and smiled reassuringly, as if thinking the same thing.

"Melanie cracked her head open at school at the beginning of the semester," Ben volunteered. "She was unconscious and an ambulance drove into the quad and they put her in the hospital and everything."

"How did that happen?" Traci asked, finally interested in something Ben had said.

Melanie seemed embarrassed. "It was a stupid accident," she explained, looking down at her lap. "A cheerleading stunt that never should have happened."

"You're a cheerleader?" Traci asked.

"Yes. But now that we have a real coach, things have gotten safer."

"Melanie's one of the *best* cheerleaders," Jenna put in, thinking her friend too modest. "She's co-captain of next year's squad."

"Really?" Traci smiled nostalgically. "I was a cheerleader too. Isn't it the best?"

Melanie glanced at Nicole, who was staring off into the woods as if suddenly fascinated by trees.

"It's okay," Melanie answered uneasily.

"Just okay? I thought it was the best thing about being in high school! I *loved* it. Especially cheer camp—cheer camp's the absolute best. Are you going to camp this summer?"

"Um, yeah. It looks like it."

"You don't sound very excited," Traci said incredulously. "I'll bet you've never been before, right? You are going to have a *blast*. Just you wait and see."

Before Melanie could reply, Nicole stood up abruptly, a tragic look on her face. "I forgot I have . . . I have to . . . back in a minute," she squeaked, running off toward the cabin.

Traci watched her go with a slightly alarmed expression. "Is she all right?"

"Not really," Melanie said. "She didn't make the squad."

"Oh, no!" Traci squeezed her eyes shut. "Oh, I feel awful."

"I'll go get her," Jenna said, starting to rise to her feet.

"No, I'll go," Melanie said. "Just . . . go on ahead without us. You can tell us what we miss later, Jenna."

"I will," Jenna promised, vowing to concentrate extra hard.

Melanie took off after Nicole.

"Poor Nicole," said Leah. "Every time it seems like she's getting over it, something happens."

"I am so sorry," Traci repeated. "I wish I'd known."

"It's not your fault," Peter said quickly.

"You can't always get what you want," Jesse added, staring after Melanie. "Besides, it's only cheerleading."

"It's only cheerleading to *you*," Jenna said. "It's important to Nicole."

"Well, Melanie's talking to her now, so she ought to be all right. Maybe the rest of us ought to get back to business," Leah suggested.

"Yeah, if we don't want to be here till midnight," said Jesse.

"If that's what you all think . . . ," Traci said uncertainly.

"Yes. We should go on," Jenna said. Despite his

199

rudeness, Jesse had a point. At this rate, how was anyone going to get certified before summer?

"All right, then," Traci said, returning to her manual. "Before we get into the specifics of care, we should take a minute to talk about disease control. These precautions are meant to protect the victim as well as the rescuer, and they're mostly common sense. Obviously you want to avoid touching anything bloody if you possibly—"

"Oh!" Ben shouted, leaning forward. "This one time, when I was five . . ."

Jenna sighed and leaned back on her bench. *It's a good thing summer's still a few weeks away.*

Miguel hesitated outside the hospital Wednesday afternoon, his backpack over his shoulders and his heart up in his throat. The week Dr. Wells had given him to make his decision was over, and however much he might have wished to avoid going into the building, he knew the moment had come. It was time to get it over with.

I'm ready, he thought, feeling faintly nauseous. *I can do this.*

With a couple of deep breaths, he crossed the remaining pavement to the lobby, went through the doors before he could think, and crossed straight to the elevator.

All I have to do is go down to Personnel and sign some papers, he thought, finger hovering over the Down button. *I can be out of here in five minutes without seeing anyone I know.*

He took another shaky breath and pushed the Up button instead. The door whooshed open instantly, as if someone had kept the elevator waiting there just for him. Miguel stepped inside, doing his best not to panic.

I can ride straight past. I can go up to the roof. No one knows I'm coming.

His finger pressed the 2.

The elevator doors opened onto a busy scene in the children's ward. There looked to be two or three families in the waiting room, and some obviously healthy siblings of patients were tearing the playroom apart. Only one harried nurse was behind the desk, but she took the time to smile as he walked by.

"Hey, Miguel."

"Hey, Tina," he returned, not stopping for conversation.

The nurses' lounge was empty, except for the ever-present smell of coffee and a clutter of unfinished paperwork. A pile of charts was spread out on one table, as if someone had begun working on them and then been called away. Aside from that, everything looked exactly as Miguel had left it. He checked his cubbyhole and found a half-finished time sheet and some picture books—exactly as he had left it. It seemed impossible that nothing had changed, but not a thing in the room was different.

Except for me. I'm different, he thought, slipping his backpack off his shoulders.

Unzipping it slowly, he removed his blue uniform top and shook out the wrinkles. His mother had washed it for him and pinned his name tag back to the front: MIGUEL, STUDENT VOLUNTEER. He stared at the words a long, long time, then pulled the top on over his T-shirt.

Reaching into his backpack again, he retrieved a decrepit paper bag and carefully extracted its treasure: a green Wildcats baseball hat. He kissed it for luck, then put it on his head, making sure the strap was secure. He was stashing the rest of his stuff when Howard walked into the lounge.

"Hey, Miguel," the senior nurse said, as if not in the least surprised. "You working today?"

Miguel smiled appreciatively at Howard's nonchalance. They knew each other well enough not to make an embarrassing scene.

"Yes," he said, taking one last deep breath. "I'm ready now. Who needs me?"

"Where is she?" Nicole muttered. "Come on! The suspense is killing me."

The note had come during fifth period: Sandra wanted to see her in the gym at four o'clock. Since then, Nicole's curiosity had been unbearable, and the minutes since school had let out had been the most excruciating of all. Now she rocked back and forth on the lowest gym bleacher, as if the motion could make the seconds tick faster.

What does she want? she wondered for the thousandth time. *Could Melanie have talked to her?*

The timing did seem suspicious, since she'd just been crying on Melanie's shoulder again the afternoon before. Maybe if Traci hadn't gone on and on and *on* about cheerleading camp and how Nicole was missing the time of her life . . . After all, she was only human.

On the other hand, if crying is all it takes, I'd have gotten on the squad a long time ago. Nicole sucked in a breath at the thought. *Don't assume you're getting on. You don't have any idea why she wants you. Don't set yourself up by thinking you're going to get on.*

But of course that was *all* she could think. Why else would Sandra have called her?

Dear God, let that be it. Please, God, let that be it, Nicole prayed fervently, rocking double time.

A door shut at the end of the gym, making Nicole's eyes fly open. She sprang shakily to her feet, wiping sweaty hands down her dress as Sandra came over the polished floor.

"Hello, Nicole," she said, glancing at the caged clock on the gym wall. "You're right on time."

Nicole smiled uncertainly, not knowing if it would help or hurt to tell Sandra how early she'd been.

"Well, you've probably guessed why I asked you to meet me," Sandra continued bluntly. "We had an unexpected drop on the squad today, and we'd like you to fill the position. Are you still interested?"

"Am I!" Nicole gasped, so thrilled she felt dizzy. The whole gym seemed to spin around her.

"Are you okay?" Sandra asked.

"Yes. Fine. I'm great!" she got out, fighting to regain her breath. "I'm just so happy—and so surprised! I thought I would never get on."

Sandra's expression turned slightly sour. "Quite honestly, I didn't expect to have an opening. But apparently not everyone on the squad was as dedicated as I thought." She gave Nicole a piercing look. "I hope *you* take this commitment seriously and make cheering your first priority."

"I will!" Nicole promised. "Oh, you bet I will! This is the best thing that's ever happened to me."

Sandra smiled and began removing some photocopied pages from her clipboard. "Well, one person's loss is another's gain. I have some information here to help you get up to speed. It's too bad you missed the first meeting, but I'll make sure to introduce you at the next one. In the meantime, you'll need to go get measured for your uniform and give them a deposit check. There's the address," she added, pointing, "and don't put it off, because the other girls' uniforms are already ordered."

"I won't." Like she would even dream of postponing!

"It's too bad you can't just take the one that's already paid for, but there's no way it'll fit you, so that's not an option."

"That's okay," Nicole said quickly. She didn't want someone else's uniform—even if it *was* brand new. She wanted one made especially for her. "I don't mind being measured."

Sandra nodded. "Fine. The other thing we have going right now is summer cheerleading camp. I don't have any more color brochures, but here are some black-and-white copies. The other girls are studying them too, and soon we'll decide which camp to go to and when, so we can get our reservation."

"Camp is going to be so fun," Nicole breathed, remembering what Traci had said. "I can't wait!"

"I'm glad you're excited," said Sandra. "Keep that enthusiasm high, and you'll do just fine."

"Oh, I'm enthusiastic," Nicole assured her. "I'm *way* enthusiastic."

For the first time that afternoon, Sandra gave her a genuine smile. "It's good to have you aboard, then. I know this must have been a bumpy ride, being the runner-up and all, but those finals were so close, and to judge everything on just one performance . . . another day, things could easily have gone differently. You deserve to be on the squad, and once we start working I know you'll prove that."

"I will!" Nicole promised, nodding. "I'll work

harder than anybody—twenty-four/seven if I have to. You'll see."

"I'll look forward to it," said Sandra. "All right, then. There's a sheet somewhere in that stack with the date of our next squad meeting. I'll see you there."

"See you there!" Nicole repeated happily as Sandra began to walk away.

She was in! It was official, and the gym was finally slowing its rotation. She still couldn't believe someone had been stupid enough to drop, but that was their problem, not hers.

"Hey, Sandra," Nicole blurted out impulsively. "Who was it? The person who dropped, I mean."

Sandra turned back around, the sour look on her face again. "Melanie Andrews."

"Melanie?" Nicole gasped, stunned.

"I wouldn't have expected it from her either." Sandra shook her head. "You just never know about people, I guess."

"But Melanie was dedicated," Nicole protested. "She's *totally* dedicated!"

"Apparently not. I really have to go now."

The cheer coach turned and strode off across the basketball courts, shoes squeaking with each step. Nicole watched until Sandra was out of sight, then sank onto a bleacher, dazed.

How could Melanie have quit the squad? Melanie, of all people?

Nicole had no sooner asked than she knew.

She did it for me, she realized, overcome with both gratitude and a deeper emotion, one she couldn't quite describe. *Melanie only dropped out to make a place for me!*

Find out what happens next in Clearwater Crossing #16, *Tried & True*.

About the Author

Laura Peyton Roberts is the author of numerous books for young readers, including all the titles in the Clearwater Crossing series. She holds degrees in both English and geology from San Diego State University. A native Californian, Laura lives in San Diego with her husband and two dogs.

Get a Life

When a classmate is diagnosed with leukemia, the students at Clearwater Crossing High organize a fund-raising carnival. But after they've formed teams to work the booths, the members of one group find they couldn't be more different. There's aloof Melanie, the girl who has it all . . . and wannabe Nicole, who wishes she did. Best friends Peter and Jenna jump at the chance to make a difference, while football jock Jesse sees a perfect opportunity to impress. Brooding Miguel keeps to himself . . . to the frustration of confident Leah. And tag-along Ben? He just wants to make some friends.

Soon the carnival is over, and the surprisingly close-knit team members drift back to their regular lives. Then an unexpected tragedy strikes. Will the eight friends come together again . . . or is it time to say good-bye?

Clearwater Crossing #1, *Get A Life*, is
on sale now from Bantam Books

0-553-57118-4

Reality Check

Jenna and her friends are having a car wash to help needy kids. There's more in the autumn air than soapsuds, though. . . .

Leah and Miguel are trying to keep their new love a secret . . . but a heartbroken Jenna is the first to find out. And if her over-before-it-began romance isn't bad enough, her younger sister Maggie is driving her crazy! How can Jenna have a life when she's sharing a room with the enemy?

Peter's got a crush too—on Jenna! He doesn't want to ruin the special friendship they share. Is telling her the truth the answer?

Nicole's determined to win a national model search. It would be sweet payback to conceited Jesse for humiliating her at school. But payback doesn't quite fit with Nicole's resolution to be a better person—does it?

Clearwater Crossing #2, *Reality Check*, is on sale now from Bantam Books

0-553-57121-4

Heart & Soul

A fter a cheerleading stunt goes terribly wrong, Melanie is rushed to the hospital. Her frightened friends are praying for her recovery. Drifting in and out of consciousness, she feels a comforting presence. Is her imagination at work, or is Melanie not as alone as she thinks?

Of course Nicole is concerned about her so-called friend, but she has a modeling contest to worry about. She's still following a strict diet—she's got to be in perfect shape. Especially now that Jesse's begun to take her seriously.

Jenna finally has a room she can call her own! She loves its privacy, its spaciousness. But will her new surroundings cause hurt feelings between Jenna and her closer-than-close sisters?

Clearwater Crossing #3, *Heart & Soul*, is
on sale now from Bantam Books

0-553-57124-9

Promises, Promises

Halloween is around the corner, and Eight Prime is putting in a lot of hours working on a spooky haunted house fund-raiser. It's the perfect opportunity for Leah and Miguel to bring their budding relationship into the open. So what is Miguel so afraid of?

Jesse's off the football team—maybe forever. If he can't convince Coach Davis that he's given up drinking, he can give up his NFL dreams for good. Jesse's ready to promise the coach anything to get back on the Wildcats. But promises can be hard to keep....

Melanie would never have believed she'd be interested in a do-gooder like Peter. Yet lately he's the only thing she thinks about. Not that she's falling for him, or anything dumb like that. She and Peter would make a terrible couple. Wouldn't they?

Clearwater Crossing #4, *Promises, Promises*, is on sale now from Bantam Books

0-553-57127-3

Just Friends

Bonfires, pep assemblies, and *football*: Spirit Week has kicked into high gear at Clearwater Crossing High! All Nicole can think about is getting Jesse to take her to the homecoming dance, but he's not in a partying mood. Nothing matters now that he's off the Wildcats.

Everything matters to Jenna these days. Dealing with her sisters, earning good grades, getting over Miguel . . . more than ever, Jenna needs a friend she can count on. She needs Peter. But has her best friend in the world found someone he likes better?

Ben is on a mission—to fit in! He thought being part of Eight Prime would solve all his problems, but he's still invisible at school, and his new friends don't really seem to accept him. Then Ben hits on a plan. If he can pull this off, he'll be the toast of CCHS!

Clearwater Crossing #5, *Just Friends*, is
on sale now from Bantam Books

0-553-49258-6

Keep the Faith

Ever since her mom's death, Melanie has dreaded the holidays. This year, though, she's got to put on a happy face: Amy, one of the underprivileged children she's been a friend to, is spending Thanksgiving weekend with her!

When a kidney becomes available for Miguel's ailing mother, he drops everything to be by her side. In a moment of desperation, he vows he'll do anything, *anything*, if only his mom will get well. Will Miguel have the chance to make good on his promise?

Now that Eight Prime is *this* close to buying a school bus for needy kids, there's no further reason for them to stay together. Nicole's ecstatic: She's free! At last she can go back to her regular life. The funny thing is, she doesn't really want to anymore. . . .

Maybe achieving their goal isn't the end . . . just the beginning of everything else.

Clearwater Crossing #6, *Keep the Faith*, is
on sale now from Bantam Books

0-553-49259-4

Everyone has
their own path
to follow. . . .

New Beginnings

laura peyton roberts

New Beginnings

Amid the hustle and bustle of preparing for Christmas, Nicole can barely find a moment to breathe. She can't wait for winter break—until her parents drop a big bombshell. . . .

Melanie's last-minute holiday plan is just a teensy bit complicated. First, she needs to keep it secret from her dad, and second, the scheme involves a major-mileage road trip. Will Jesse's sleek BMW come to her rescue?

Peter and Jenna have dreamed up the best gift ever: winter camp for the Junior Explorers. But the fun stops short when an Explorer disappears . . . and Eight Prime must find the child before it's too late.

Clearwater Crossing #7, *New Beginnings*, is
on sale now from Bantam Books

0-553-49256-X

One Real Thing

Not only did Melanie fail to set things right with her family, she did what she swore she never would: She let Jesse into her life. Now that she's opened the door, slamming it shut could prove to be a losing move.

Ben's never kissed anyone . . . and it's starting to really bother him. He's determined to get his first smooch by the new year's end. How hard can it be?

Leah's got to make up her mind whether or not she'll compete in the national finals of the modeling contest she reluctantly entered. Being in front of the camera isn't her thing, but she can't turn down a chance at a scholarship and a free trip to California with her friends. Can she?

Clearwater Crossing #8, *One Real Thing*, is
on sale now from Bantam Books

0-553-49257-8

Skin Deep

Good-bye, Clearwater Crossing . . . hello, California! Well, at least for the weekend. The girls of Eight Prime are on an all-expenses-paid trip to the Golden State, and each of them has her own agenda. . . .

Leah's trying to focus on the modeling competition—and the scholarship that goes with it. But how can she strut down the catwalk when all she can think about is Miguel's marriage proposal?

Melanie's ready for sunshine and fun, forbidding herself even a moment's thought about Jesse. So why is it that everywhere she looks she sees his face?

Jenna's squeezing in as many cool sessions as possible at the Hearts for God youth rally. She wants Nicole to join her, but her starstruck friend is too busy keeping her eyes peeled for movie stars—and hoping to be discovered. Will Nicole give faith a chance . . . or is Hollywood calling her name?

Clearwater Crossing #9, *Skin Deep*, is
on sale now from Bantam Books

0-553-49260-8

No Doubt

Every time Jenna gets involved in Caitlin's life, she makes things worse. How could she have revealed her shy sister's crush on Peter's handsome brother? And now that she has, how can she earn back Caitlin's trust?

Just because she got in a little trouble, Nicole's parents have found her a job—at the restaurant where her perfect cousin, Gail, works. Nicole is less than thrilled to be around such a Goody Two-shoes until she discovers that Gail isn't quite as good as she remembered . . . or as all the adults seem to think.

In an unguarded moment, Miguel proposed to Leah. He'd have said anything to keep from losing her. But now that she seems on the verge of accepting, he's on the verge of panicking. Is marriage really the answer?

Clearwater Crossing #10, *No Doubt*, is
on sale now from Bantam Books

0-553-49261-6